An Inner Darkness

Look for these titles by
Ally Blue

Now Available:

An Inner Darkness

Ally Blue

A Samhain Publishing, Ltd. publication.

Samhain Publishing, Ltd.
577 Mulberry Street, Suite 1520
Macon, GA 31201
www.samhainpublishing.com

An Inner Darkness
Copyright © 2009 by Ally Blue
Print ISBN: 978-1-60504-331-9
Digital ISBN: 1-60504-227-7

Editing by Sasha Knight
Cover by Anne Cain

First Samhain Publishing, Ltd. electronic publication: October 2008
First Samhain Publishing, Ltd. print publication: August 2009

Dedication

As always, love, hugs and a huge collective "thank you" to the girls in my crit group. Y'all are wonderful friends as well as wonderful critique partners and I love you all madly! Mwah! Also, my eternal gratitude to Sasha, my editor, who has held my hand through the entire BCPI series and helped keep me sane. I heart you, lady!

Chapter One

"Happy birthday, dear Sean, happy birthday to you."

The song ended and the group burst into applause as Sean Broussard blew out the nine candles on his cake. He grinned, big hazel eyes shining at his family and friends gathered around the kitchen table.

Sam Raintree watched with a smile. The boy's obvious joy made the effort of being civil to his mother worthwhile.

As if he'd sensed Sam's thoughts, Sean's father, Dr. Bo Broussard, turned and met Sam's gaze. Sam gave his lover a wide grin. Bo grinned back before turning to cut his son's cake.

"Give Sam a corner, Dad," Sean instructed. "He likes lots of icing."

"I know." Bo arched an eyebrow at Sam. "Sam has very strange tastes sometimes."

From somewhere to his right, Sam heard a faint snort. He glanced over at Janine, Sean's mother, who was standing a few feet away wearing the big fake smile she'd had plastered on her face ever since she and her boyfriend, Lee Rogers, had arrived. Her gaze met Sam's, and her smile faltered. For a second, hatred blazed in her eyes. Then she turned away, the corners of her mouth hitching up again as her bland mask slipped back into place.

Sam swallowed a sigh. She was trying, for Sean's sake, just as they all were. He knew she was. But her feelings were crystal clear. She hated Sam just as much now as she had when she'd first learned he was the reason Bo had left her.

When he thought about it, Sam supposed it was a minor miracle that the three of them had managed to be in the same room for almost an hour already without one insult being hurled at anyone. Of course, it might've been a different story if they hadn't all promised Sean an argument-free birthday party with his whole family and all his friends together.

Sam smiled to himself. Only Sean could sweet talk people who hated each other into spending an afternoon together without fighting.

Bo held out a plate with an icing-laden corner slice on it. "Here, Sam."

Moving to Bo's side, Sam took the plate and picked up a red plastic fork from the pile beside the cake. "Thanks." He leaned closer and lowered his voice. "So far, so good, huh?"

"Yes, thankfully." Bo handed two plates to his oldest son, eleven-year-old Adrian, who stood silent and sullen beside his father. "Take these to your mom and Lee, okay?"

Adrian gave him a baleful look, but did as he was told. Sam watched as he handed Janine and Lee their cake. Janine's smile morphed into a more genuine one, though the expression in her eyes was guarded. She thanked Adrian and patted his head, which Sam knew Adrian detested. Lee took his plate with a muttered thanks. His expression was tight, his discomfort with Adrian clear. Even after six months with Janine, he always seemed to wear that look around Adrian, and it hurt Sam's heart to see it.

His own relationship with Adrian had never been easy, but he had to give himself credit for the effort he'd put into getting along with the child. Lee never seemed to try very hard, at least as far as Sam could see, and Janine didn't even seem to care. Adrian was a smart boy, every bit as intelligent and observant as his father. He must've felt Lee's uneasiness around him, and his mother's apathy toward that fact. He was already struggling to come to terms with his parents' divorce, his father's homosexuality, and having Sam in his life. How hard must it be for him to live with a stranger who didn't like him on top of everything else?

Bo's hand on the small of his back brought him out of his thoughts. He blinked and focused on Bo's face. "Sorry, was I zoning out?"

"Yes." Bo took Sam's arm and steered him into the open kitchen on the other side of their small apartment. "Is everything all right?"

That was their secret code for "what's Janine done now?" Nodding, Sam set his untouched cake on the counter. "Everything's fine."

Bo didn't look convinced. "What were you thinking about?"

"Nothing."

"Sam."

"Really, it was nothing."

Bo crossed his arms and leveled an "I know better" look at Sam. Sam sighed. "Okay, I was thinking about Adrian. He's having such a hard time adjusting to everything. I just wish Lee would make more of effort with him, and I *really* wish Janine would at least pretend she gives a damn."

"She does. It just doesn't always show on the outside." Bo's lips curved into a humorless smile. "You know better than probably anyone else how difficult Adrian can be when he sets his mind to it, and he makes things even worse for Lee than he does for you. You don't see it like I do, since you don't go with

11

me to pick up the boys at Janine's and take them back again, but it's true."

A familiar resentment swelled in Sam's chest. "I'd go with you if she'd let me." Even though he wasn't particularly anxious to spend more time with Janine, it still rankled that she ended up throwing Sam off her property every time he tried to go over there with Bo.

"I know you would." Bo's fingers wove through Sam's. "And I know it seems like Lee isn't trying, but he is, really. He just needs more time."

"Yeah, I guess you're right." Sam glanced at the group around the table. Sean was laughing with his friends, cake crumbs clinging to his chin and a smear of blue icing decorating his cheek. Adrian stood a little apart from the rest, silent and glowering, his arms crossed over his chest like a shield. "He looks exactly like you—hell, he *is* exactly like you in most ways—but he reminds me so much of myself at that age. I just wish he'd let me help him."

Sam wasn't certain how to help Adrian, or what exactly he wanted to help him with. All he knew was that he couldn't bear to see a child looking as alone and out of place as he himself had once been, and he wanted to make it better if he could.

Bo squeezed Sam's hand. "You're a good man, Sam. The boys and I are lucky to have you in our lives. One day, Adrian will realize that."

"I hope you're right. I don't want him to hate me forever. It's too damn hard on all of us."

"I'm right. You'll see." Smiling, Bo tugged Sam toward the birthday crowd. "Come on. Sean'll be ready to open presents soon."

Sam let himself be led back into the thick of the party. For a second, Adrian's gaze met his. He smiled at him. Adrian held

Sam's gaze for a heartbeat before turning away.

It wasn't exactly a declaration of undying affection, but it was as close as Adrian had ever come to being friendly to Sam. Right now, that was good enough for him.

∞

After the cake was eaten and all the presents opened and exclaimed over, Sean and his friends decided to go outside and play on the jungle gym in the backyard of the converted mansion where Sam and Bo's apartment was located. Watching the gang of youngsters from the back porch swing, Sam thanked his lucky stars once again that he and Bo had been able to stay in the same building when they switched apartments back in April. With only one bedroom, Sam's old place had been too small to accommodate the boys when they came for their every-other-weekend visits with their father, but neither Sam nor Bo had wanted to leave the lovely old house. The large, shady backyard with the jungle gym and playhouse was only one of the reasons they wanted to stay. The vacancy on the third floor had come at the perfect time, and they'd snapped it up the minute the building's owner informed them it was available.

Sam drew a deep breath of fragrant autumn air. The mid-October day was warm and sunny and the yard rang with laughter. Away from Janine's accusing gaze, he felt lazy and content.

He looked up when the back door squeaked open. Adrian stormed out and kicked the door shut with a bang that shook the walls. He stomped across the porch and stood at the top of the steps with both small fists clenched tight, glaring at the back fence as if it had done something horrible to him. He didn't seem to have noticed Sam sitting in the swing in the shadows at the edge of the porch.

Sam didn't much like trying to talk to Adrian when he was like this, and he knew Adrian wasn't any more fond of it than he was. But the longer he sat there and said nothing, the angrier Adrian would be when he found out Sam had been sitting there watching him all along.

Here goes nothing. Sam cleared his throat. "Adrian?"

The boy's head whipped around, sending a hank of his overlong black bangs flying into his eyes. His face twisted into a scowl when he spotted Sam. Lips pressed into an angry line, he shoved his hair out of his face and started toward the back door again.

Acting on pure instinct, Sam stood and took a step toward him. "Are they fighting again?"

The expression that crossed Adrian's face told Sam he was right. He bit back a sigh. It wasn't the first time Janine and Bo had gotten into a screaming match, nor was it the first time one or both of the boys had witnessed it. They tried to keep their interactions civil in front of the kids—or at least Bo did, Sam had his doubts about Janine—but there was still a great deal of anger and resentment between them, and sometimes it came out in less than ideal ways.

Reclaiming his spot on the swing, Sam gestured to the empty space beside him. "You want to sit out here for a while?"

Adrian hesitated. He glanced from Sam to the back door and back again. With a shrug, he shuffled over and plopped down on the swing, as far away from Sam as he could get.

They sat in silence while Sean and the other boys chased each other across the yard in some wild game only they understood. Sam stole a sidelong glance at Adrian. He sat with his arms crossed over his belly, head down, frowning at the

14

blue-painted boards beneath his feet. Something about him seemed different, though Sam couldn't put his finger on it.

"So." Sam cast around for something to say that wouldn't destroy the fragile peace between them. He couldn't think of anything, so he asked the question uppermost in his mind at the moment. "What're your mom and dad fighting about this time?"

To Sam's surprise, Adrian let out a harsh laugh. "Me and Sean. What else?"

"What? Is your—" Sam cut himself off before he could ask if Janine was trying to screw Bo out of visitation again. No matter how much he might hate the woman sometimes, he refused to say anything against her in front of her sons.

Adrian shot him a glance far too bitter and knowing for an eleven-year-old. "No."

Sam waited. Adrian scowled at the ground.

After several seconds of mental back-and-forth, Sam decided to go ahead and ask. "So what is it?"

"I told you."

"You told me they were fighting about you and Sean. You didn't tell me what exactly it was."

Adrian darted a fierce glare at Sam from beneath his bangs. "It's none of your business."

If Bo had heard Adrian speak to Sam in such a way, he would've berated the boy. Sam couldn't bring himself to do the same. He could hardly blame Adrian for resenting him.

Turning sideways and curling one leg beneath him, Sam studied Adrian's profile. Adrian was a child who appreciated honesty. Maybe telling him the truth would earn his respect.

"I understand why you think it isn't my business," Sam said, keeping his voice low and even. "Maybe you're right. But I

15

love your father. I plan on being with him for the long haul. You and your brother are more important to him than anything else in the world, and that makes you both important to me." He risked a slight smile. "Besides, the more I get to know you and Sean, the more I like you."

"Everybody likes Sean," Adrian muttered, kicking the toe of one black sneaker against the floor.

Sam didn't contradict him. Insulting Adrian's intelligence by trying to pretend what he'd said wasn't true wouldn't endear Sam to him.

"He's a likeable kid. But so are you. You're just harder to get to know, that's all. I'm kind of that way myself." Sam started to reach out and touch Adrian's arm, then thought better of it. "I know it must be pretty rough getting used to everything that's going on. If you want to talk, I promise to listen, and help you if I can."

Adrian fixed Sam with a penetrating stare so like Bo's it gave Sam chills. Sam gazed back, doing his best to look calm and relaxed. The silence hung heavy and charged between them. The laughter and shouting in the yard seemed far away.

Hanging his head, Adrian studied the hole in the knee of his jeans. "Dad was mad at Mom because..."

He trailed off. Sam waited.

"She said..." Adrian glanced at Sam from beneath a curtain of dark hair, and this time the misery and apprehension in his eyes was crystal clear. "She wants to—"

The back door banged open. Janine strode out in a palpable fury. "Sean," she called. "Lee and I are leaving now. Come say goodbye."

Sean's head poked out from behind the gigantic oak tree in the back corner of the yard. He dashed across the grass, barreled up the steps and flung himself at his mother so hard she staggered backward a couple of steps. "Bye, Mom," he said, small arms squeezing her tight.

"Bye, baby." She leaned down and kissed the top of Sean's head. "I love you."

"Love you too." He tilted his head up to give her a questioning look. "Where's Lee?"

"Waiting in the car. I'll tell him goodbye for you."

"'Kay. Thanks." Grinning, Sean let go of Janine, waved at Sam and Adrian and plunged back into whatever game he and his friends were playing.

Janine turned toward the swing where Adrian and Sam sat watching her in silence. Her shoulders were tight, the warm smile she'd worn for Sean nowhere to be seen. "Adrian? Come give me a hug?"

For a moment, Adrian just stared at her with such contempt Sam almost felt sorry for her. Then he shrugged, pushed to his feet, walked over to his mother and gave her a perfunctory hug.

Janine put her arms around her son and kissed his hair. "I love you, honey."

If Adrian noticed the slight quaver in her voice, he gave no sign of it. "Me too. Bye."

Adrian drew out of Janine's embrace, went to the door and disappeared inside. Sam sat still and silent in the swing, trying to be invisible. Dealing with Adrian was hard, but they were making progress. Dealing with Janine was a fucking nightmare, and that hadn't changed one bit.

Unfortunately, she had no apparent intention of leaving without one of her usual cutting speeches. She crossed her arms and pinned Sam with the cold, haughty glare that always made him want to punch her in the face. "What are you doing hiding out here? Pouting because Bo's not paying attention to you right now?"

Sam regarded Janine with as much calm as he could muster. "Someone needed to watch the kids."

"Oh, are you already bored with fucking my husband? Moving on to the next perversion?"

Sam shut his eyes and drew a deep, slow breath. *She's trying to goad you into losing your temper. She's looking for an excuse to keep the boys away from you and Bo. Don't let her.*

Opening his eyes, Sam pinned her with an ice-cold look. "First of all, he's not your husband anymore. He and I are together now, and it's about time you accepted that." She flinched, and he felt a surge of dark satisfaction. "Second of all, you know damn well I'd never even *think* of a child that way." He rose to his feet, hands tucked into the back pockets of his jeans to keep them from balling into white-knuckled fists. "Lastly, what Bo and I have together is good, and above all it's normal. I don't ever want to hear you call our relationship 'perverted' again."

She sneered, eyes glittering with a malevolent light. "Or what? You'll give me a nice set of scars to match Bo's?"

That one hit hard. Even though Sam knew he wasn't to blame for either of the times the otherdimensional creatures wounded Bo, he still felt a vague sort of guilt over it. He wasn't entirely sure why, though he suspected his psychic connection to the portals and the things on the other side had something to do with it.

Not that Janine knew any of that. Nor would she ever, if Sam had anything to say about it. She just liked to blame Sam for everything bad that had happened in the past year. He understood that, in a way. His struggle for perspective when it came to Janine was an ongoing one.

Sam drew himself up as straight as he could. "Believe it or not, Janine, I don't want to fight with you. I'd much rather we at least tried to get along with each other. If you want an argument, go pick one with Lee. I'm done."

He didn't stop to see the murderous expression he knew would be on Janine's face. Pivoting on his heel, he stalked down the steps into the yard and stood watching the boys play.

After a few seconds, he heard the back door open and close. When he turned to look, Janine was gone.

Chapter Two

Bo came outside ten minutes after Janine left. He leaned against Sam's shoulder. "Sam, I'm an idiot."

"Only sometimes."

"Smartass."

Sam slipped his arm around Bo's waist. "Why are you an idiot?"

"For letting Sean talk me into having this damn party." With a deep sigh, Bo rubbed a hand across his forehead. "I knew better. I knew it would end badly. I just couldn't tell him no."

"Well, at least you and Janine didn't start yelling at each other until Sean and his friends were outside, so the party wasn't ruined for him. I think he got what he wanted." Sam rubbed his fingertips in soothing circles against Bo's hip where his hand rested. "What were y'all fighting about?"

"How'd you know we were fighting?"

"Adrian told me. But I would've assumed you'd fought anyhow. You always do."

Bo let out a harsh laugh. "I wish you were wrong, but you're not."

"So what was it about?"

For a few moments Bo was silent, staring out at the yard

where his youngest child was playing. When he spoke, his voice was soft and sad. "She tried to take the boys back home with her and Lee."

Sam tightened his arm around Bo and counted to ten in his head. "She and Lee took Sean out for a birthday dinner last night, plus they got to come to the party here. It's your weekend to have the kids. She *knows* that. What the hell's her problem?"

"Honestly? I have no clue. I'm tempted to say she hates us, but I don't think that's it."

Sam snorted. "Well, she's doing a great imitation of hating us, then."

"Yes, but I just don't think that's it."

"Maybe she's just homophobic."

"No, I don't think that's it either."

Sam gave Bo an incredulous look. "Are you serious? After all the things she's said about us being perverted?"

"Well, yes, I know she spouts off all the time about the evils of homosexuality, but I don't think it's that so much as the fact that she essentially lost out to you. She hasn't had any real feelings for me for years now, she just hates to lose what she sees as hers to someone she thinks doesn't deserve to have it."

It made sense. Sam nodded. "Okay, I can buy that."

Sighing, Bo snuggled closer to Sam's side. "I guess I shouldn't have lost my temper with her in there, but *God* she makes me so fucking angry."

"What did you say to her?"

"I told her it was our weekend with them and I wouldn't let her take them. She trotted out all the usual arguments and threats, and I dug out the papers we'd both signed allowing me to keep the boys every other weekend and waved them in her face." Bo snorted. "It sort of went downhill from there."

"That explains why she was so furious this time. Not that she isn't always."

Bo turned to look at Sam with a frown. "Did she say something to you?"

"She implied that I'd corrupted you with my evil gay ways, that our relationship is sick and perverted, and that I'm responsible for your past injuries." Sam gave Bo a grim smile. "Just the usual."

Bo did not look amused. "And what did you say?"

"I told her that you and I are together now and she'd better get used to it, and that I never wanted to hear her call us perverted again." Sam scratched his chin. "I probably shouldn't have reminded her that you're not her husband anymore. It just pissed her off even more. But it just sort of came out."

"I'm sure she loved that."

"Oh yeah."

At that moment, Sean detached himself from the huddle of children and ran over to Bo and Sam. "Dad, I wanna go get pizza! Can we?"

Laughing, Bo ruffled Sean's hair. "Didn't you just have pizza last night?"

"Yeah, but it was at that fancy place Mom likes." He wrinkled his nose. "It had peppers and mushrooms and those are *gross*. I like just plain pepperoni." Grabbing Bo's shirt in both hands, Sean gazed up at him with a pleading expression. "I wanna go to Pizza Palace Arcade and drive the car! Please, Dad?"

Sam stifled a laugh. Every time the boys came over, Sean begged his father for a trip to the huge new Pizza Palace on Airport Road. He'd fallen madly in love with the simulated race car game in the restaurant's gigantic arcade.

"All right." Bo patted Sean's cheek. "After the party's over and your friends have gone home, we'll get the apartment cleaned up, then we'll go to Pizza Palace for dinner. Okay?"

"Okay. Thanks, Dad." Beaming, Sean bounded across the yard to rejoin whatever game he and the other boys were playing.

"You're so easy," Sam murmured, sliding his hand down to give Bo's ass a quick squeeze. "He gives you that little puppy-dog look, and you just cave."

Bo arched an eyebrow at him. "Pot. Kettle."

Sam had to laugh. He was no more immune to Sean's sweet-faced wheedling than Bo, and they both knew it. Drawing away from Bo, Sam took his hand and laced their fingers together. "The kids'll be out here playing for a while. Let's sit in the swing."

"I think that swing is the main reason you wanted to stay here," Bo observed, grinning.

"Maybe." Sam gave Bo's hand a tug. "Come on."

With an amused shake of his head, Bo followed Sam toward the porch. Just before they reached the steps, Sam glanced up at Sean and Adrian's bedroom window, which overlooked the backyard. A dark head ducked out of sight.

Adrian. Watching them again. When that happened, it usually meant a difficult weekend ahead. Though he never came right out and said it—probably due to a justifiable fear of punishment—Adrian hated seeing Sam and Bo show any sort of physical affection. The slightest brush of hands was enough to send the boy into a simmering fury for days at a time.

It was the main reason weekends with the boys seemed to Sam to last forever. He was used to being able to touch Bo as much as he wanted when they were at home. To hold him, kiss him, make love to him. Adrian's glowering presence kept Bo at a distance, and Sam hated it, even though he'd come to care a great deal for the child.

"Sam?" Bo moved in front of him as they reached the top of the steps. His brown eyes radiated concern. "Are you okay? You were a million miles away just now."

Shoving away thoughts of Adrian and Janine and anything else that could cast a pall on the remainder of the day, Sam smiled. "I'm fine." He grabbed both of Bo's hands and pulled him to the big wooden swing. "Let's make out. No one's watching."

Chuckling, Bo sat beside Sam, their thighs pressed together. One swift, chaste kiss was all Bo allowed, but his hand remained firmly clasped in Sam's. It was enough.

$$\infty$$

Sam woke with a start, heart racing. He glanced at the bedside clock. Two a.m. Beside him, Bo lay sprawled on his stomach, sound asleep. Whatever had woken Sam, it evidently hadn't disturbed Bo at all, and he was a light sleeper.

Sam sat up, listening as hard as he could. The only sounds were the faint hum of the refrigerator and the occasional rumble of a car passing outside. *Must've been another dream.* He didn't remember having one just before waking, but he didn't know what else it could've been. Nothing stirred in the apartment, and the psychic feelers he sent out detected nothing out of the ordinary.

Sam slipped out of bed and padded out into the short hallway, pulling the door closed behind him. Experience had taught him that he wouldn't be able to go back to sleep until he'd checked the whole apartment to make sure nothing was amiss. Silly, he knew, but he couldn't help it.

The living room was empty and quiet, as were the kitchen and the bathroom. Sam opened the door to the boys' bedroom as quietly as he could, slipped inside and peered around. A yellowish glow from the floodlight outside seeped through the curtains, lending a dim illumination to the room. Sean lay on his back in one of the twin beds, arms and legs flung outward as if to take up as much space as possible. The covers were balled at the foot of the mattress. In the other bed, the top of Adrian's head poked out from under the blanket swaddled around his curled form. Both children appeared to be fast asleep.

It was just a dream that woke you, looks like. Reassured, Sam turned and tiptoed out of the room. Now that he knew everything was okay, drowsiness was already overtaking him. He yawned.

Just as he was about to shut the door, a faint noise floated from the boys' room. Sam froze, listening. The sound came again, a faint scraping like metal against wood. Tendrils of fear crept up Sam's spine and down his limbs. His mouth went dry, his heart thudding so hard and fast it made him dizzy.

Gathering all his courage, Sam pushed the door wide and stepped into the bedroom. At first, nothing seemed out of place. Then he noticed Adrian had shifted positions. One arm now lay bent beside his head, the hand resting palm up on the edge of his pillow. The shark's tooth necklace Bo had bought him the last time they visited the beach swung back and forth from where it hung on the bedpost. Adrian's fingers curled just beneath the swaying pendant. He shifted and mumbled in his sleep.

Sam leaned against the wall, weak with relief. Adrian's hand must've hit the necklace when he moved and set it swinging. What Sam had heard was simply the sound of the shark's tooth rasping across the wooden bedpost.

The adrenaline drained from Sam's body, leaving him shaky and exhausted. Exiting the room for a second time, he closed the door and shuffled back into his and Bo's bedroom. He fell into bed and wrapped his arms around Bo, molding himself to Bo's back. Bo muttered something unintelligible and wriggled deeper into Sam's embrace, then lay still again with a soft sigh.

Sam buried his face in Bo's neck and shut his eyes, but sleep was a long time coming. When he finally drifted off, his dreams were filled with darkness and terror, and the click of obsidian claws.

∞

Sunday dawned cloudy and cold. Bo, Sam and the boys spent most of the day watching movies and finishing off the rest of the birthday cake. After dinner, Sean and Adrian gathered their things and Bo drove them back to their mother's house. To Sam's surprise, Adrian offered him a handshake and a solemn goodbye before leaving. For Adrian, it was equivalent to the rib-cracking hug Sam always got from Sean. That one simple gesture nearly canceled out the lingering bitterness of Sam's confrontation with Janine the day before.

Sam spent the rest of the evening in high spirits. He was still practically floating when he and Bo arrived at the Bay City Paranormal Investigations office at eight forty-five Monday morning.

Danica McClellan, the company's latest addition, glanced up from the pile of paperwork on the reception desk with a smile as Sam and Bo entered. "Hello, Bo, Sam."

"Good morning, Danny." Sam flung his arms outward as if trying to hug the whole office at once. "What a *gorgeous* day."

David Broom leaned backward in his chair to peer through the front window at the rain pounding outside. "Um. Yeah." He grinned, blue eyes sparkling. "Bo, what'd you do to him this morning? Whatever it was must've been pretty good if he's this happy on a Monday morning."

"David, really." Cecile Langlois, who'd been dating David for just over a year, patted his balding head as she rose from her desk and crossed to the coffee maker at the back of the room. "When are you going to learn not to ask?"

Laughing at David's apprehensive expression, Bo shut the umbrella and dropped it into the plastic bucket they kept beside the door. "Don't worry, it's nothing like that."

"Adrian said goodbye to me last night." Still grinning, Sam shrugged out of his jacket and hung it on the coat rack, where it dripped water into the puddle already on the floor. "I know it's not much, but usually he either ignores me or gives me the evil eye, so I felt like it was progress."

Cecile gave him a wide smile. "That's great, Sam."

Rising from her seat, Danny walked around the desk and kissed Sam on both cheeks. "What a step forward for you both. I'm very happy for you."

"Thanks." On impulse, Sam pulled her into a tight hug. He'd liked her from the minute she'd first walked into the office to apply for the job of receptionist-slash-office assistant. She looked reserved and conservative, from the close-cropped, graying Afro to the dark business suits and sensible shoes, but she was an Earth Mother at heart. She'd already converted Cecile to vegetarianism and had come close to talking David into it as well before he balked.

27

With a soft laugh, Danny patted Sam's back and drew out of his embrace. "Bo, you have an appointment at nine," she said as she returned to her work. "He called just this morning."

Bo tossed his jacket onto the coat rack and moved over to lean against Danny's desk. "What kind of case?"

"A potential haunting. Quite an active one, from the sound of it. The man was very anxious to talk to you."

David let out a whoop. "Cool."

"What's cool?" Dean Delapore wandered in from the bathroom at that moment, drying his hands on a paper towel. He tossed it in the trash can and plopped into his chair. "Hey, y'all."

"Hi." Bo scanned the piece of paper Danny handed him. "There's a Mr. Jones coming in in a few minutes with a haunted house case for us."

Dean's eyebrows went up. "We're paranormal investigators. Checking out haunted houses is pretty much what we do. *All* our cases are cool."

"Yeah, but Danny said this one sounded really active." David shot Dean a dimpled grin. "We haven't caught anything good on camera since Fort Medina. I'm looking forward to catching some footage we can put on the website."

"Assuming the client will give us permission to publish our findings online." Bo glanced at Danny. "Do you know if Andre will be here in time to sit in?"

Sam looked around, belatedly noticing that Andre Meloy, co-owner and manager of the business, was nowhere to be seen. Not that it was entirely unusual. Andre often came in around midmorning and stayed until late in the night working.

"He should be, yes. He usually lets me know when he's going to be late and he hasn't said anything."

As if in response to their conversation, the door swung open and Andre walked in. He nodded at the group. "Hi."

Everyone called hellos and good mornings. Skirting Danny's desk, Sam sat down and booted up his computer. "Hey, Andre. We're getting a new haunted house case."

"We still need to talk to the guy before we decide whether or not to take the case." Bo clapped Andre on the shoulder. "The client's coming in at nine to talk to us, can you sit in?"

"Sure." Unzipping his black raincoat, Andre slipped it off and hung it on the rack with the other coats and jackets. "What information do we have?"

"Nothing yet," Danny answered. "The gentleman said he'd rather discuss it in person."

"Okay." Andre glanced at the clock. "Looks like I have time for a cup of coffee."

"That sounds good." Sam gave Andre his most winning smile. "I could use some myself."

Andre smirked as he passed Sam's desk. "You should probably get up and pour yourself a cup then."

Shaking his head, Bo followed Andre to the coffeepot. He poured some of the fragrant liquid into the Ghostbusters mug Sam kept at the office, stirred in a little of the powdered chocolate creamer sitting on the counter and brought the mug to Sam. "Here. Anyone would think you didn't have three cups at home just an hour ago."

"But it tastes so much better when someone brings it to me," Sam said, straight-faced.

Bo laughed. He bent to press a light kiss to Sam's lips, palm stroking Sam's hair as he straightened up again. "Andre, when Mr. Jones gets here, bring him on in, will you?"

"Sure thing."

With a nod at Andre and a smile for Sam, Bo turned and sauntered into his office. Sam propped his chin in one hand and watched the hypnotic sway of Bo's hips. The man was sex on legs. Every time Sam looked at Bo, he couldn't help feeling a sense of profound gratitude that this incredibly sexy, beautiful, fascinating man was his lover. Their life together might not be perfect, but the sense of intimacy and belonging he'd found with Bo was worlds above what he'd ever thought he would have. They were happy, and that was all Sam needed.

The sound of the front door opening shook Sam out of his thoughts. Tearing his gaze from the open door to Bo's office, he clicked open the document containing the paperwork he was still finishing on the last case. He and Bo were pretty much out as a couple now, but the sight of an employee gazing moon-eyed at his boss did not tend to inspire confidence in new clients.

"Good morning," Danny greeted the person who'd just walked in. "Can I help you?"

"I have an appointment with Bo for nine o'clock. I'm afraid I'm a little early."

Sam went still. He knew that voice. Had heard it just two days ago, at the most uncomfortable birthday party he'd ever attended.

Half afraid to look, he turned his head, and met the nervous gray-eyed gaze of Lee Rogers.

Chapter Three

Sam was up and walking around Danny's desk before he even realized it. "Lee? *You're* 'Mr. Jones'?"

Lee took a step backward at Sam's approach, but held his gaze without flinching. "I was afraid Bo wouldn't see me if he knew I was...well, me."

Behind Lee, Bo emerged from his office. "I wouldn't have turned you away, Lee. We're in the business of helping people. That doesn't in any way exclude people with whom we have some sort of personal relationship, no matter what that relationship might be."

Lee's long, thin face went faintly pink. "I didn't mean to imply otherwise," he said, turning as Bo walked up to him. "I'm sorry for the deception. I guess I wasn't thinking straight."

"Don't worry about it." Smiling, Bo gestured toward his office. "Have a seat in my office. Would you like some coffee?"

Lee nodded. "That would be great, thanks."

Danny stood. "I'll get it. How do you take your coffee, Mr...?"

"Rogers," Lee supplied. "Lee Rogers. Just a little sugar, please."

"Thank you, Danny. Andre, could you join us?" Bo glanced at Sam, an apology in his eyes, and Sam felt a rush of affection.

Bo was all business when it came to BCPI, but he never failed to spare a thought for Sam's feelings, and he had to realize Sam was dying to know what had brought Lee here. The "haunted house" story had to be a front. It couldn't possibly be the real reason for Lee's visit.

"I think Sam should be in on this too, since if you take my case you'll have to deal with Janine and the kids. Is that okay?" Lee took the mug Danny handed him and smiled his thanks.

"Of course he can sit in, if you like." Bo started toward the office. "Danny, I think it would be a good idea if you hold my calls during this meeting. Except in case of an emergency, of course."

"Certainly."

Sam trailed behind Bo and Lee. Andre stepped into Bo's office beside Sam. They shared a questioning look. Everyone in the BCPI office knew Lee's name, but no one but Bo and Sam had ever met him. He'd never been to the office before. Sam wondered what was so pressing that he would risk Janine's wrath by coming here.

The four of them settled into the comfortable leather chairs gathered around Bo's desk. Lee took a sip of his coffee. His hands trembled ever so slightly.

"So. Lee." Arms folded on his desk, Bo leaned toward Lee. "What can we help you with?"

Lee frowned. "I told your secretary when I called. We have a haunting."

A muscle twitched in Bo's jaw. "I'm sorry, I'd assumed you'd given Danny a false reason for coming here as well as a false name."

Lee ran a hand through his shaggy brown hair. "I wish. No, I think our house really is haunted. It's nearly one hundred years old, people are bound to have died there in the past. I've tried to find some other explanation for what's been happening, something *normal,* but nothing else fits." He let out a harsh laugh. "Janine's going to kill me when she finds out I came here. She doesn't exactly believe in the supernatural. But I'm sure you knew that already."

Clasping his hands in his lap, Andre fixed his sharp brown-eyed gaze on Lee. "Tell us what's been going on in the house, and for how long."

"I've lived there for four years, but never experienced anything out of the ordinary until about three weeks ago, about a month after Janine and the boys moved in. Strange noises, lights going on and off, objects falling off shelves for no obvious reason. Nothing spectacular, for the most part. Certainly nothing you couldn't blame on other, more logical explanations if you tried hard enough." Lee's brows drew together in a troubled frown. "Until last night."

"What happened last night?" Bo asked, watching Lee's face.

Lee shifted in his chair. "It was about an hour after you dropped the boys off. They were getting ready for bed, and Janine and I were talking." He grimaced. "No, that's not true. We were arguing. I lost my temper and yelled at her. Things were just starting to get really ugly, when I felt an intense, burning pain in my back, right between my shoulder blades. It hurt so badly it stopped the argument cold. Janine had me take my shirt off so she could look, and she found four shallow parallel scratches right where I'd felt the pain a moment before."

Sam felt his eyes widen. "Wow."

"Yes." Lee gave Sam a humorless smile. "Of course, Janine thought I must've scratched myself earlier, and not noticed until that moment. But I know that wound wasn't there before. It happened when we were fighting, and no one was in the room but Janine and me. And there was nothing inside my shirt that could've caused those scratches. It almost has to be something paranormal that did it." He turned his pleading gaze from Sam to Bo to Andre. "This all started out slowly, with just a few strange noises and such, but it's escalating fast. The boys are getting scared. Can you help us?"

Bo sighed. "You haven't spoken with Janine about this yet." It wasn't a question.

Lee shook his head. "No. That's one of the things I wanted to discuss with you. How do we talk Janine into allowing BCPI to investigate our house?"

"Let me talk to her," Andre volunteered. "Bo, I know you'll want to go, but I think having me there to act as a buffer between you would be good. Maybe she'll be more willing to listen that way."

Bo nodded. "Yes, she probably would. Good thinking."

"Why BCPI?" Sam blurted out. Three pairs of eyes turned to Sam in surprise. "There are a couple of other paranormal investigation firms within reasonable driving distance," he explained. "Wouldn't it be better to hire one of them, considering how Janine feels about us? About me in particular?"

"No, I don't think so. Janine will object regardless, and I don't believe any other company will handle this situation with the sensitivity it needs."

Bo frowned. "I'm not sure what you mean."

Hunching his shoulders, Lee stared at the coffee stain on Bo's desk. "What's happening seems to be affecting Adrian in a really negative way. I mean it's frightening both of the kids, but it's hitting Adrian particularly hard. Not that he talks about it. He hasn't said a word. But he's been unusually restless and distracted lately. And what happened to me last night really upset him."

Sam raised his eyebrows. "Don't take this the wrong way, but I was under the impression that Adrian didn't like you much more than he likes me."

"He doesn't," Lee confirmed. "He wasn't solicitous or openly concerned about my wellbeing. He seemed angry, actually, but terrified at the same time. I heard him last night, pacing the living room, and he was up before dawn this morning. It was pretty obvious he didn't sleep much, if at all. Something about what's happening at the house is affecting him in a deeply personal way, and he won't let me close enough to figure out what it is."

"And Janine scoffs at the whole idea of any sort of phenomena outside of current scientific understanding. She always has, even when we were together. Adrian won't be likely to turn to her for help." Bo drummed his fingers on the desktop. "I think I see why you want us to do this. If Adrian won't trust you or Janine with what's bothering him, maybe he'll trust me, since obviously I'll listen to what he has to say and hopefully be able to give him some sort of understanding of what's happening at your home and how to cope with it."

"That was my thought exactly." Lee glanced from Bo to Sam, his expression cautious but hopeful. "So, will you take the case?"

"Of course we will," Bo answered without hesitation. Standing, he stretched his open hand across the desk. "I'm glad you came to us."

Clearly relieved, Lee rose to his feet and shook Bo's hand. "Me too. Thank you."

"We'll need a few more details about the case, and you'll need to set up a time for Andre and me to go with you and talk to Janine." Bo let go of Lee's hand and turned to Andre. "Andre, do you have time to talk with Lee for a few minutes and get that information?"

"Sure." Andre pushed out of his chair. "Lee, is now good for you or do you need to come back later?"

"Now's fine."

"Okay, good. We can sit down in the back room, it's a little more private." Andre headed for the door, gesturing for Lee to follow. "Come on."

Lee nodded to Sam and Bo as he trailed Andre out of the office. The minute they were gone, Bo strode over and shut the door, then threw his arms around Sam's neck.

Taken by surprise, Sam held Bo close, cheek pressed to his hair. Bo's body shook in his arms. "Bo? You okay?"

"No."

Bo's voice was muffled against Sam's neck, but Sam heard the tremor in it. He rubbed a hand up and down Bo's back. "Are you worried about the boys?"

"Yes." Bo drew back enough to meet Sam's gaze. "I hate not being able to see them but every other weekend. And now they're experiencing things that have to be terrifying to them, and their own mother doesn't even believe it's real. I should be there for them, especially now, and it kills me that I can't. It fucking *hurts*."

Wanting to soothe away the pain in Bo's deep brown eyes, Sam cupped Bo's cheek in one palm and kissed him. The sweet, familiar sigh Sam loved slipped from Bo's lips as they parted for Sam's tongue.

"It'll be all right," Sam whispered when the kiss broke. He ran his thumb over Bo's plump lower lip. "Sean and Adrian know how much you love them. They know you're always there for them when they need you."

"I always thought so. God knows I've tried to show them

that." A vast sadness welled up in Bo's eyes. "But neither of them has ever said a word about this. Not one word. Why is that, if they really trust me to listen to them and help them? Wouldn't they have told me?"

"You know how Janine is about stuff like that. She probably already has them trained never to mention it. She's probably told them it's their imagination and threatened to punish them if they say anything."

"I guess."

Bo didn't sound as if he believed it. Right then, Sam hated Janine more than he ever had.

Picking up Bo's waist-length black braid, Sam pulled it over Bo's shoulder and let it run like a thick, silken rope through his hand. "You know I'm right. Sean and Adrian both adore you. They're always excited to be with you, and you know as well as I do that they both confide in you way more than they do in Janine. Remember last month, when Sean told you about his 'girlfriend' and didn't tell Janine? Or when Adrian asked for your help with his science project because, and I quote, 'you're better at that stuff than Mom'? Or when they got up early and made you breakfast in bed for your birthday?"

Bo's eyes narrowed. "You're trying to make me feel better."

"Everything I just said is perfectly true."

"Sam."

"Okay, so I'm using the truth to make you feel better." Sam grinned. "Is it working?"

"Yes." A soft smile curved Bo's mouth. "You're quite an observant guy, Sam."

"I am. Keen eye for detail and all that."

"Hm. I see." Bo kissed Sam's throat, his chin, the corner of his mouth. "Can your keen eye observe how grateful I am to have you in my life?"

"Definitely." Sam let out a breathy moan as Bo's lips brushed the shell of his ear. "And the feeling is mutual, by the way."

"Good." Drawing back, Bo gazed straight into Sam's eyes. "Thank you, Sam. I really do feel a lot better about things now."

"I'm glad."

"Kiss me again?"

Smiling, Sam tilted his head and met Bo's lips with his. Bo melted against him, fingers buried in his hair.

In the back of his mind, Sam knew the upcoming case would be one of the most difficult they'd ever tackled, and not for any of the usual reasons, but he couldn't be bothered to worry about it. Not now. Not with Bo in his arms, kissing him with a passion that made his knees weak.

Tomorrow, they'd face what they needed to face, together. Right now, everything was just as it should be.

Chapter Four

Sam glanced at the time display on his computer monitor. Six fifteen. More than two hours since Bo and Andre had gone to help Lee break the news of the investigation to Janine.

"They should've been back by now," Sam said, swiveling his chair to frown at the closed front door of the BCPI office. "It ought not to take this long."

"Which 'they'?" David asked without turning from the case report he was typing.

Dean and Cecile were out doing a follow-up visit to the site of a previous case—a poltergeist haunting, the first real one Sam had ever seen—and had yet to return. Danny had gone home an hour ago, leaving Sam and David alone in the office. David had been hard at work on his case report ever since, and the lack of conversation was doing not a damn thing to calm Sam's frazzled nerves.

"Bo and Andre." Sam glanced at his case report, still open on the computer screen. He needed to finish the thing, but he couldn't keep his mind on it. "I wonder what's going on?"

"They're dealing with Janine," David reminded him. "You know she's going to be as big a pain in the ass as she can."

"I know." Sighing, Sam stood and walked over to the refrigerator in the corner. "You want a drink?"

"We got any Mountain Dew?"

Sam checked. "Yeah." He pulled out a can for David and grabbed a bottle of grapefruit juice for himself. "I wish I could be there. This waiting's killing me."

"Look at it this way. If she'd just said 'no way' right off the bat, it wouldn't be taking this long." David took the can Sam held out to him. "Thanks."

"Sure." Sam plopped into his chair, twisted the cap off the juice bottle and took a long swallow. "God, I hope she doesn't try to keep me out of this case."

"She'll try."

"You're not helping."

With a put-upon sigh, David saved his report, closed the document and spun his chair around to face Sam. "Seriously, Sam. What're you gonna do if she lets us investigate, but only on the condition that you're not there? And don't tell me that won't happen," he added, cutting off Sam's protest. "Because we both know it might."

Sam shook his head. "Bo won't let her do that."

"Bo might not have a choice." Leaning forward, David rested his elbows on his knees and pinned Sam with an uncharacteristically serious look. "This is about his kids. I know he loves you, and he'd want you there in any case because you're an important part of the team. But if the only way for him to help his kids is to leave you out of it, I'm thinking he'll agree to that. He won't like it, but he'll do it."

Sam scowled at the plastic bottle clutched between his hands. David was right. As much as Bo loved Sam and respected his work, if it came down to a choice between doing the investigation without him or not doing it at all, he knew which one Bo would choose.

The front door squeaked open. Sam looked up, hopeful, and couldn't help deflating a little when Dean and Cecile walked in. "Hi, guys."

"Hey." Strolling around behind Danny's desk, Dean gave Sam a questioning look. "Bo and Andre aren't back yet?"

"No," David answered. He took Cecile's hand and kissed it as she walked over to him. "How was the follow-up?"

"Fine. The incidents have decreased since the daughter started therapy, so it looks like we were right about her being at the root of it." Cecile glanced between David and Sam with a frown. "What's going on?"

"Nothing. We were just talking." Sam gave her a wan smile. "Or to be more exact, I'm worrying myself sick over what exactly is happening right now with Janine."

Nodding, Dean plopped into Danny's chair. "That explains the lack of enthusiastic greeting when Cecile and I walked in. You were wanting to see Bo."

Sam shrugged, feeling sheepish. "Kind of, yeah."

Dean clutched dramatically at his chest. "Geez, Sam. Break my heart, why don't you?"

Sam had to laugh. "Wonder what Kyle would say to that?" Dean had been dating Kyle DuPree ever since they'd met at the beach back in May. It was the longest Dean had ever been with any one lover in the eleven months or so Sam had known him.

Sadness fleeted through Dean's eyes and was gone before Sam could decide if he'd really seen it or not. "We broke up."

Sam blinked. "Oh. I'm sorry."

"Naw, it's okay. Kyle was great, but nothing lasts forever, right?" Dean jumped to his feet, his smile a little too wide to be real. "Okay, I guess I'm heading out. See y'all tomorrow."

They all called goodbyes as Dean sauntered out the door

with a wave. David shook his head. "I'd say he needs to get laid, but he already gets laid too much as it is."

"He needs a relationship that'll last, and that's something he has to be ready for before it'll ever work." Cecile bent and kissed the top of David's head. "Are you almost finished with your case report? We should head home ourselves." Straightening up, she turned to Sam. "Unless you want us to stay with you and wait?"

He did, but he wasn't about to say so. David and Cecile had worked just as long a day as he had, and were no doubt anxious to get home. He wasn't about to keep them from their private time out of a selfish wish for someone to keep him company while he worried out loud.

"No, y'all go on. I'll be fine." Sam gestured toward the half-finished report still open on his computer screen. "I have to finish this anyhow."

David shut down his computer, stood and flashed Sam a teasing grin. "Next time maybe you'll finish up your work like *some* of us did instead of sitting over there stewing in angst."

Sam snorted. "Ass."

"Oh, so *that's* why you're so anxious for Bo to get back. You want some *ass*." David slugged Sam in the shoulder. "You horn dog."

"David, stop being childish." Moving to Sam's side, Cecile took his hand and squeezed it. "Are you sure you're okay alone, Sam?"

Before Sam could answer, the door banged open, making all three of them jump. Bo stormed in, cheeks red and eyes snapping. "One day, that *fucking* woman is going to drive me around the *fucking* bend."

"So it didn't go well, huh?" David guessed.

"It could've been a lot worse, really. She's just so damn frustrating." Sighing, Bo perched on the edge of Danny's desk and rubbed a hand over his eyes. "God, I'm tired."

"We can head on home, if you want." Setting his partially finished juice beside his computer, Sam stood, leaned over the desk and started massaging the tension out of Bo's upper back. "I'm almost done with my case report. I can finish it up in the morning."

Bo gave Sam a wan smile over his shoulder. "I'd like that."

"Aren't you going to tell us what you worked out with Janine about the investigation?" Cecile frowned. "And where's Andre?"

"He dropped me off here and went on. He promised to baby-sit for his sister tonight." Bo shifted sideways to face Sam. "We're starting the investigation at Lee and Janine's place on Friday night. Sean and Adrian are both staying over with friends that night. We'll go back on Monday during the day, when the kids are in school."

David's eyebrows went up. "So she only wants us to be there when the boys aren't?"

Bo grimaced. "Sort of."

An ugly feeling settled in Sam's gut. He suspected David was right, and Sam himself was the main reason Janine didn't want the boys around during the investigation.

Cecile cleared her throat. "Okay. Well, David and I are going home. See y'all in the morning."

Sam murmured his goodbyes along with Bo. David clapped Sam on the shoulder before grabbing his jacket and following Cecile outside. The door clicked shut, leaving Sam and Bo alone in a heavy silence.

"Are you going to tell me what she said?" Sam asked when

Bo failed to offer any information.

"She doesn't want you around the boys during the investigation." One corner of Bo's mouth hitched up in a bitter smile. "Unfortunately, I know that's no surprise to you."

"No, it isn't." Rising to his feet, Sam walked around the desk and pulled Bo up as well. "What do we have to work with here? Am I even allowed to participate?"

"Yes."

Sam blinked, surprised. "Really?"

"Yes, really." Bo let out a sharp laugh. "If Janine had had her way, you wouldn't be. But I told her we need the full team, which I believe we do, and Lee backed me up."

"So what are the limitations?"

"She agreed to let you come with us Friday night, but that's it so far. I asked Lee to talk to her and try to convince her that I want you with us on this because you're an important part of the BCPI team, not because you're my lover. He said he'd try." Bo wound his arms around Sam's waist, his expression apologetic. "I'm sorry, Sam. I would've changed her mind if I could, but you know there's only so much I can do. It *is* her house. Well, half hers, anyway."

"I know." Forcing a smile, Sam looped his arms around Bo's shoulders and pulled him close. "Hey, at least I'm going the first night. That's more than I expected, to be honest."

"Lee's a good influence on her." Bo tilted his head to plant a kiss on Sam's lips. "When we were married, she never would've given even an inch. I got the distinct feeling the only reason she did this time is because Lee wanted her to."

"Hm." Sam returned the kiss, with a hint of tongue this time. "I may have to reevaluate my opinion of the guy."

"I agree." Bo pressed closer, his thigh sliding between

Sam's legs to lodge against his groin. "Let's go home, Sam. It's been a long day, and I really just want to curl up in bed with you right now."

"That sounds like a plan to me." Sam rubbed his crotch on Bo's leg. "You want to stop and get take-out, or you want me to make soup and sandwiches?"

Bo's hand slid into Sam's hair. He pressed his cheek to Sam's. "Grilled cheese? With tomato?"

"Of course." Sam tilted his head sideways so Bo could kiss his neck. "I know how much you love grilled cheese and tomato sandwiches."

"Mmmm." Bo's tongue traced the shell of Sam's ear. "It's so sexy when you cook for me."

"Probably because I hardly ever do it." Groaning, Sam snagged Bo's braid in one hand and tugged him away. "You'd better stop, unless you're up for a quickie on your desk."

An evil grin spread across Bo's face. "Well, I *do* have lube in the drawer."

"Oh, my God." Planting his hands on Bo's shoulders, Sam held him at arm's length. "You have lube in your desk drawer? Seriously?"

"Yes."

"Damn." Sam laughed. "We've been together a whole year now, but you still surprise me."

Bo's eyebrows went up. "Is that good?"

"Definitely." Sam leaned in for a quick kiss, then stepped back. "Come on, let's go home. I'd much rather you fucked me in our bed than across your desk."

"Truthfully, I agree with you." Bo grabbed Sam's jacket from the coat rack and handed it to him. "We can use my desk another day."

"Oh, yeah. I'm not forgetting about *that*, what with the lube in the drawer and everything."

Bo snickered, and Sam grinned. It was good to see Bo relaxing a little after the confrontation with Janine. It could've gone much worse, but the whole thing had clearly been stressful for Bo. Seeing some of the tension leave Bo's face made Sam happy.

Sam retrieved his juice bottle, then followed Bo outside. Bo locked the door behind them. As they descended the porch steps, Bo slipped his hand into Sam's. "I know how much you must hate having to sit out the field portion of this investigation. Thank you for being so understanding about this."

Sam squeezed Bo's fingers. "It's fine, Bo. I don't mind."

The look in Bo's dark eyes said he knew better, but he didn't say anything, for which Sam was grateful. They were lucky Janine had agreed to the investigation at all. He didn't like being left out, but there wasn't much point in saying so. If it would help Bo help his sons, then Sam would do as Janine wanted and keep his complaints to himself.

For now, anyway.

∞

The rest of the week flew by in a blur of phone calls and paperwork. Friday night arrived before Sam was ready for it. Standing on the front steps of the early twentieth-century house where Lee, Janine and the boys lived, Sam promised himself for the umpteenth time that he would remain calm and polite no matter what Janine said or did. He was a professional, and by God he intended to act like it. He would be the mature one if it killed him.

Which it just might, he thought glumly as the front door swung open to reveal Janine on the other side.

Beside Sam, Bo tensed. "Hello, Janine."

"Hello, Bo. Everyone." Shooting a hard glare at Sam, she stepped back and swung the door wide. "Come in."

They all filed through into the cozy foyer. Dean stopped beside her, beaming as if there was nowhere he'd rather be than standing beside the grim-faced woman. "Thank you, Janine. It's all right if I call you Janine, isn't it?"

Janine blinked at him. "Yes, of course. That's fine."

"Excellent." Dean leaned against the doorframe, his eyes shining with a near-painful sincerity which Sam knew for a fact was completely false. "I'm thrilled to be here tonight, Janine. Thank you for having us here."

Looking flustered, Janine fiddled with the tiny gold cross hanging around her neck. "Um. You're welcome." She glanced toward the stairs rising from the back of the foyer. "Oh, here comes Lee."

Sam fought back the urge to laugh at the relief on Janine's face. He knew how she felt. When Dean turned on the charm, it could be a little overwhelming. Sam wondered what Janine would say if she knew Dean was just doing it to throw her off balance.

"Hi, guys," Lee called as he descended the last few steps. He shook hands with each of them in turn, a wide smile on his face. "I'm so glad you could do this. I'm anxious to get to the bottom of whatever's going on here."

Bo's smile looked almost normal. "So am I, Lee. Hopefully we'll be able to find an explanation for the unusual events here. This is such an old house, some of what you've all experienced will almost certainly have a more mundane cause than paranormal phenomena."

"Meaning old houses creak a lot and tend to have noisy plumbing." David set the camera case he was carrying on the floor and turned to Bo. "So. Where do we start, boss-man?"

"Before we do anything else we need to tour the house and see the spots which are the most active paranormally speaking. Andre and I can do that while the rest of you unload the equipment and set up the computer." Bo looked over at Lee and Janine, who stood side by side at the bottom of the staircase. "Is that all right with y'all?"

Lee nodded. "That's fine. Janine and I can show you the house and point out all the places where we've experienced strange things."

Janine crossed her arms. "Well, since I haven't experienced any of these so-called phenomena myself, I can't very well show you anything. I think I'll just stay here and keep an eye on things while you show them around, Lee."

The cold glare Janine leveled at Sam told him he was in for another of her venomous tirades the moment they were alone. He suppressed a sigh. At least the kids weren't around to witness any of it this time.

Before Sam could decide what—if anything—to say, Bo moved to his side. "I think you should come with Lee, Andre and me," Bo told his ex-wife, a clear warning in his voice. "You might not have seen anything yourself, but that doesn't mean you don't have any information we can use."

Janine's eyes narrowed. Sam cut her off before she could start the fight she obviously wanted. "It's okay, Bo. We'll be fine."

Bo turned to meet Sam's gaze. Seeing the question in Bo's eyes, Sam gave him a nod and a faint smile. He wasn't looking forward to whatever Janine had to say, but he'd deal with it. If he kept his cool and refused to rise to her bait, maybe they could even agree on a truce or something. God knew he was sick of fighting with her.

To Sam's surprise, Bo took his hand, pulled him close and planted a light kiss on his lips. It was swift and chaste, but it was a bold move considering that Bo had never kissed Sam in front of Janine before. Sam wondered why he was doing it now, of all times.

Facing Janine, Bo pinned her with a hard stare. "I want you to listen to me," he said, each word clipped and careful. "We are all here tonight in a professional capacity, and that includes Sam. Whatever your personal feelings might be, you need to put them aside and let us do our job."

Janine sneered. "I never wanted you here in the first place."

"But I did, and this is my house as much as it is yours." Lee slipped an arm around her shoulders. "Just...be nice, okay? For me. Please."

Janine's cheeks went red. She glared up at Lee. For a second, Sam thought she was going to chew Lee out. Then her expression softened. "Don't worry, honey. Go give Bo and Andre the grand tour."

"Thank you, sweetheart." Smiling, Lee kissed the top of her head. "Okay. Bo, Andre, why don't we start upstairs? The boys' rooms seem to be the most active spots."

"All right." Bo squeezed Sam's hand before letting go. "Andre, could you bring your video camera, just in case? I'll take notes."

Andre patted the camera bag slung over his shoulder. "I'm on it."

"Great, thanks." Bo plucked a small spiral notebook and pen from his back pocket. "Let's get going. The rest of you set up what you can, but wait on the cameras until Andre and I get back. We'll let you know the best spots for those."

Sam watched Bo and Andre trudge up the stairs behind Lee. He wished he could go with them. No matter what implied promises she'd given Lee, Sam didn't trust Janine to keep the peace.

As if in response to his thought, she stalked over to him and leaned close, hands clasped behind her back. "I see you can't stop staring at Bo. Not terribly professional, Sam. Do you always think about sex when you're supposed to be working?"

Sam shut his eyes. God, he was sick to death of her digs. Why couldn't she just leave him alone? Especially now, when she and Lee seemed to be happy together.

Struck by a sudden inspiration, Sam opened his eyes and met Janine's angry glare. "Why do we have to be enemies, Janine?"

Her eyes went wide. "Are you kidding?"

"No, I'm not." Sam glanced around the room. David and Cecile had left to start unloading the SUV. Dean was busy setting up the laptop on the dining table in the next room. "Look, I know we're never likely to be friends. I know you don't like me, and I can't blame you for that. But why do we have to be enemies? There's no reason for it."

"You destroyed my marriage," she spat. "You broke up my family. My children have been through hell this past year, because of *you*. Give me one good reason why I shouldn't hate you for that."

Sam fought back the evil urge to remind her how she'd propositioned at least one of Bo's friends while they were still married. "I'm truly sorry for everything Sean and Adrian have been through. I know it doesn't really matter now, but I never set out to break up a family. But you never would've found Lee if it hadn't happened." Sam touched her arm, willing her to listen to him. "Bo's happier now. *You're* happier now. And even though the boys have had a tough time of it, they're coming around. Why can't you and I at least try to get along?"

Janine's lips pressed together in a thin line. She turned away and walked toward the front door, the set of her shoulders announcing her tension to anyone who cared to look. "I'm going out. Tell Lee I'll be back later."

She snatched her purse from a hook on the wall, yanked the front door open and strode out into the night. David and Cecile, coming in through the door at the same time, hurried to get out of her way.

"What the fuck's *her* problem?" David grumbled, shuffling across the room with four bags full of power cords.

Sam let out a dry laugh. "She's going out."

Shaking her head, Cecile bumped Sam's arm with hers as she followed David to the spot beside the stairs where he'd dropped the heavy bags. "At least she won't be hanging over our shoulders. I think we'll all be more relaxed without her here."

She was right, much as Sam wished she wasn't. He was so tired of fighting with Janine. Whenever she was around, he felt as if he were tiptoeing over broken glass, and he was sick of it.

When Cecile went to help David get out the cameras and cords, Dean strolled over and stood staring at Sam with a solemn expression.

"What?" Sam snapped.

Dean's eyebrows went up. "Little tense there, Sam?"

"You could say that." Running a hand through his hair, Sam plopped onto the bottom step. "I'm sorry, Dean. You know how she gets to me. I just wish she'd let it go already."

"I know." Dean turned to look at the front door, then back

at Sam. "That was a brave thing to do, Sam. Trying to make peace with her, I mean."

Sam shrugged. "Yeah, well. Would've been great if it had worked."

"Don't give up yet. It takes time to let go of that much anger." Reaching down, Dean grabbed Sam's hands and pulled him to his feet. "Come on, I need help checking the batteries in all the gadgets."

Sam dutifully followed Dean into the dining room, grateful for the distraction. So he hadn't changed Janine's mind just yet. He'd taken the first step, and he had to admit he was proud of himself for it.

And she didn't yell or anything. In fact, she looked like she might actually be thinking about what you said.

Sam smiled. Maybe there was hope for a truce after all.

Chapter Five

Bo, Andre and Lee returned from upstairs a few minutes later. Lee glanced around the foyer as he descended the steps. "Where's Janine?"

"She went out," Sam told him. "She didn't say where."

"Probably to her friend Rita's place." Sighing, Lee skirted the bottom of the steps and gestured down the short hallway leading toward the back of the house. "Okay, Bo, I'll take you and Andre to the family room now. There've been several incidents in there."

"What sorts of incidents?" Andre asked, panning the camera in a slow circle.

"Unexplained noises. Objects moving by themselves. Some strange shadows. We all frequently feel on edge there, even Janine, though you'd never get her to admit it." Lee shrugged. "As in the rest of the house, nothing that's happened in that room has been so spectacular that you couldn't brush it off as imagination or your eyes playing tricks on you. Janine thinks the whole thing is in our heads."

Bo gave him a considering look. "I have to say, for once I hope Janine's right. I'd much rather reassure my boys that their imaginations are running away with them than to try to convince Janine she has a haunted house."

Lee let out a humorless laugh. "You and me both.

Unfortunately, I have a feeling that what we've experienced here is true paranormal activity. Things have happened far too often for me to brush it off as just imagination. I only wish I knew exactly what we were dealing with."

"That's what we're here to figure out." Glancing up from his camera, Andre touched Lee's elbow. "Let's go see the family room."

Nodding, Lee led them down the hallway. Bo grabbed Sam's hand and gave it a reassuring squeeze as he passed. Sam took the warmth of Bo's touch with him when he went back to his work.

By the time Bo, Andre and Lee returned, Sam and the rest of the team had all the equipment ready to go. David jumped up from the bottom step as the trio approached. "We're all set, Bo. Y'all know where you want the cameras?"

Bo raised his eyebrows at Andre, who shut off his video camera and sauntered over to stand beside David. "At least one camera in each room, and one in the attic. Bo's got the list of the best spots to put cameras in each room."

"I think we have enough cameras to go around," Bo mused, handing a sheet of scribbled notes to David. "Once we get them all set up, I'd like to split into three teams. One will stay and monitor the central computer, the other two will do a sweep with EMF and video. One team upstairs, one downstairs. After that, we'll switch teams and sweep again with thermal and recorders for EVP work. Sound good?"

Everyone nodded. The group broke up to begin setting up cameras. Lee followed Andre, asking questions about the investigative process.

"Lee seems really interested in everything," Sam noted half an hour later, as he and Bo headed off to begin their sweep of the downstairs areas. "It's cool that he wants to learn more about what we do."

Bo nodded. "Hopefully some of his enthusiasm will rub off on Janine."

"I'm not holding my breath."

"Neither am I. But you never know."

Sam shot him a grin. "That's what I love about you, Bo. Your penchant for unfounded optimism."

Bo smacked Sam's rear. "Okay, funny guy, let's go see what we can find in the family room, since that seems to be one of the hot spots."

Switching on the video camera, Sam followed Bo down the short hallway to where a doorless archway on their left led to the family room. "Bo and Sam, downstairs at Lee and Janine's house, nine twenty p.m. October twenty-first, two thousand and five," he recited for the record.

"There seems to be a fairly strong electromagnetic field." Bo stopped just inside the doorway and moved the EMF meter in a slow arc. "Four point oh seven here. It was three even in the foyer."

The reading wasn't dangerously high, but high enough to make Sam nervous. Especially since every portal case they'd faced so far involved an elevated baseline EMF. Not that there was any indication of there being a potential portal here.

Without saying anything to Bo, Sam relaxed his conscious mind and sent cautious psychic feelers through the house. All he felt was the vibrant life force of the people gathered here. He found not a trace of the cold, malevolent energy he'd come to associate with the inhabitants of whatever universe lay on the other side of the portals.

Opening his mind wider, he searched for the skin-tingling feel of an intelligent entity or the low electric hum of a residual haunting. He encountered neither.

Maybe it's just their imaginations after all.

Reassured, Sam walked into the room and panned the camera around the smoky gray walls. The room was small, but stylish. A huge built-in entertainment center containing a plasma-screen TV, DVD player and several other electronics took up most of the wall opposite the doorway. A squashy black leather sofa lay along the wall across from the TV, its matching chair tucked into the corner next to the door. The love seat was situated along the back wall of the room. Long, dark red curtains covered the two tall, narrow windows in the outside corner, providing the only color in an otherwise unrelieved palette of black and gray.

"Where's that go?" Sam asked, pointing to a glass-paned door in the wall on the other side of the sofa.

"The back porch. There's another door across the way, leading from the kitchen." Bo paced across the floor toward the entertainment center. "Hm. EMF's going up fast. Seven, thirteen, twenty-five…" He stopped in front of the TV, his eyes going wide. "Jesus, Sam. The EMF's skyrocketing here. Look."

Sam went to stand beside Bo and peered at the EMF display. "One hundred and twelve?" He stared at Bo, shocked. "Holy shit."

"Yeah." Setting the EMF detector on a patch of empty shelf, Bo took a small flashlight out of his pocket and switched it on. He leaned over to peer behind the TV as best he could, aided by the light's narrow beam. "There's an absolutely insane tangle of cords and power strips back here. Good lord, no wonder the EMF's so high." He emerged from the narrow space with a grin. "This could explain a lot."

Sam smiled back, catching Bo's excitement. Such a high EMF was known to cause a variety of symptoms—paranoia, nausea, even visual and auditory hallucinations. Considering Lee's assertion that many of the family's experiences had occurred right here in this room, Sam wondered if they'd found their explanation already. Except...

"What about Sean and Adrian's rooms?" Sam asked, though he hated to douse the hopeful shine in Bo's eyes. "According to Lee, those are the other hot spots."

Bo's smile didn't dim one bit. "I know. But both of their rooms are on this side of the house. Adrian's room is directly above us. Sean's is next door, and his bed is positioned against the wall separating their rooms."

"So when he's in his bed, he'd conceivably be within the area affected by the EMF leakage here." Sam nodded. "It makes sense."

Pulling the two-way radio off the waistband of his jeans, Bo thumbed it on. "Cecile, come in."

The radio crackled. "Cecile here, Bo, go ahead."

"Have you been in the boys' rooms yet?"

"We're in Sean's room now."

"Okay, listen. I need y'all to check the EMF levels very carefully, particularly in the area around Sean's bed. Same thing for Adrian's room."

"Sure thing." Another muffled voice sounded in the background. "Dean wants to know if we're looking for anything in particular."

"The EMF levels in the family room are dangerously high, centering around the entertainment center. They've got all this equipment jury-rigged to death, and it's leaking electromagnetic radiation all over the place. We're wondering if it's traveling up into the boys' rooms as well."

"Oh, my God, that could explain what the kids have

experienced."

"Yes, it could. Will y'all check that for me?"

"Of course. We'll let you know what we find."

"Great, thanks." Bo turned to Sam, brown eyes sparkling. "An electromagnetism leak is fixable. I really hope that's at the root of this whole business."

"Me too." Pointing the camera toward the back wall, Sam pulled Bo close and kissed him. "Let's finish this room and move on, huh?"

"All right." With a quick nip to Sam's bottom lip, Bo drew away and retrieved the EMF detector. "Let's go clockwise around the room from the door, then cross the porch to the kitchen. We can get readings from the porch as well."

"Sounds good."

All business again, Bo strode back to the doorway leading to the hall to begin a more methodical survey of the room. Sam followed, smiling to himself. Of all the possible explanations for the strange events in the house, a dangerously high EMF was the only one Janine would accept without argument. She might even thank them for finding it.

Janine's gratitude would, in Sam's opinion, make the whole thing worthwhile. The past several months had been painfully difficult for Bo, and Sam figured it was about time things went right for a change when it came to Bo's sons and their prickly mother.

Don't get ahead of yourself, Sam, the logical part of his mind warned. *There might be other things going on here besides the EMF. Finish the investigation before you start jumping to conclusions.*

Tamping down his optimism as best he could, Sam pulled his focus back to the job at hand.

∞

Shutting off the video on his computer, Dean leaned back in his chair and stretched. "Nothing on this one."

"Same here." Sam halted his own video and turned to face Dean, who sat at the desk beside his. "All we have left is one audio recorder and a little bit of thermal, right?"

Dean nodded. "Yep. Looks like this case might be a bust."

"God, I hope so," Sam said with feeling.

Dean laughed. "Yeah, for once I guess we all kind of hope that."

Sam slumped in his seat with a yawn. It had taken them two days—well, one and a half, seeing as how Wednesday was only half over—to go over the bulk of the video, audio and thermal from Friday night and Monday. Janine had refused to let the group come back after Monday, claiming they'd already found the cause of her family's hallucinations.

So far, the hours of tape they'd reviewed bore out Janine's opinion. They revealed nothing more sinister than one loose shutter and a couple of bats in the attic. That fact, combined with the high level of electromagnetism leaking from the entertainment center to the children's rooms upstairs, lent strength to Bo's theory that an uncontrolled electromagnetic field lay at the heart of Lee and the boys' experiences. Sam had been almost afraid to hope Bo was right, but it seemed as though he was.

Sam was relieved, and not only because it meant Sean and Adrian were in no danger after all. He much preferred Bo relaxed and happy than tense with worry over his sons.

The front door opened, letting in a blast of damp wind as

David rushed inside. "Damn, it's blowing hard out there." Shucking his jacket, David hung it on the coat rack and mopped the beaded raindrops from his face. "Y'all find anything yet?"

Dean shook his head. "Zippo. What about you, did the research turn up anything juicy?"

"Nope. That old house is as boring as they get." David crossed to the coffeepot on the other side of the room, grabbed his War Eagle mug from the shelf and filled it to the brim. He blew once across the steaming surface before taking a cautious sip. "No murders, no suicides, nothing. Only one person died there that I could find, and she went peacefully in her sleep."

Dean wrinkled his nose. "God, you're right. Dull as dishwater, as my granny used to say."

Laughing, Sam rose to his feet. "In this case, dull is good. Bo's very happy that we haven't found anything, and I for one want to keep him happy."

"I bet," David said with a smirk.

"Shut up." Sam walked over and flicked David's ear. Ignoring the resulting yelp, he poured coffee and creamer into his own mug. "The fact that no one's reported any hauntings at the house in the past, or any violent deaths which might *produce* hauntings, just makes it more likely that we're right about this being hallucinations caused by that ridiculous EMF level."

Dean rubbed his chin, a thoughtful expression on his face. "Speaking of which, what are we going to do about that? It's got to be fixed, before it starts causing real problems."

"Lee's already got an electrician coming out to take a look." Sam shrugged. "Hopefully they'll be able to take care of it."

The door opened again, admitting Danny and Bo. "Lunch is here," Bo called, holding up two rain-spattered take-out bags.

"We brought stuff for Cecile and Andre too, aren't they back yet?"

Sam shook his head. "No. Of course the place they were going to look at is all the way out in Bay Minette. The round trip plus the interview would take at least two or three hours, and if they went ahead and toured the site who knows when they'll be back."

"It'll keep, no worries." Taking the bags from Bo, Danny set them on her desk and started pulling out various sandwiches and wraps from the Cajun restaurant down the street. "David, why don't you and Sam get some drinks out of the fridge?"

David grinned at her. "Sure thing, boss-lady."

Danny rolled her eyes, but an indulgent smile tugged up the corners of her mouth. Sam snickered behind his coffee mug. Bo and Andre might run the business, but Danny ran the office, and they all knew it.

A few minutes later, the whole group sat in a lopsided circle in the space between the two rows of desks, talking while they ate. Sam munched his shrimp Po Boy, content to listen. Normally, a morning as unproductive as the one they'd just had made him feel a little cranky. This time, the lack of any paranormal findings calmed his previous tension and left him feeling happily exhausted. He tucked a foot beneath him and let the buzz of conversation wash over him.

The quiet burr of the phone interrupted David's story about the dead squirrel Cecile's cat had brought them as a present that morning. "I'll get it," Sam offered, since he'd finished his lunch and everyone else was still eating.

Reaching across Danny's desk, Sam plucked the receiver from the base and thumbed it on. "Bay City Paranormal Investigations, this is Sam."

"Yes, hello," said a clipped female voice. "I need to speak to

Dr. Bo Broussard, please."

"Who should I say is calling?"

"This is Principal Green at St. Christopher's Academy."

Sean and Adrian's school. "Okay, hang on." He covered the mouthpiece with one hand and leaned close to Bo. "It's for you," he murmured. "It's the principal at St. Christopher's."

Bo's brows drew together. "Did she say what she wanted?"

"No. She just said she needed to speak to you."

"Hm." Bo chewed his bottom lip. "Could you transfer it into my office, please, Sam?"

"Sure."

Sam waited until Bo was inside his office before transferring the call. He set the receiver back on the base and studied the closed office door, wondering why the school was calling. Sean had been reprimanded a couple of times for talking during class, but neither boy had ever been in any real trouble.

God, I hope neither of them has been hurt or anything. The sudden thought made Sam's stomach knot.

Dean nudged Sam's arm. "Hey, Sam."

"Yeah?" Sam frowned. Why hadn't the school called Janine? He knew she was their primary contact. Bo hated that. He still hadn't gotten over being relegated to the status of back-up parent.

Dean's face appeared less than a foot from Sam's. He jumped, startled, and Dean grinned. "You okay, Sam?"

"Yeah, fine." He forced a smile. "Just thinking."

"Who was that on the phone?" David asked around a mouthful of potato chips.

Sam swiveled around to face him. "Personal call."

David's eyebrows went up. "So, none of my business. Gotcha."

Pushing her chair back, Danny stood and started picking up napkins and empty sandwich wrappers. "Of course Bo's personal business is his own, David. I'm sure any of us would appreciate the same consideration."

Before David could retort, Bo's office door swung open. The second Bo strode out, Sam knew something was wrong. Bo's cheeks were red, the muscles in his jaw standing out hard and tight. Sam's insides clenched.

"Sorry, y'all," Bo said before Sam could ask him what was wrong. "But I have to go pick up Adrian from school." He lifted his jacket from the coat rack and shrugged it on. "I'll be back in a little while. I hope y'all don't mind him coming to the office with me for the rest of the day."

"Of course not." Dean shot a questioning look at Sam, who shrugged. "Anything we can do?"

"No. Thanks." Bo frowned, opened his mouth as if to speak, then closed it again. "See y'all in a little while."

He yanked the front door open and hurried outside. Sam followed without stopping to think about whether or not he should. Shivering in the increasing cold and damp, he jogged across the porch in Bo's wake. "Bo, wait."

Bo stopped. "What?"

Sam ignored the snap in Bo's voice. "What happened?"

Sighing, Bo took Sam's hand in his and laced their fingers together. "Adrian's been suspended."

Sam's mouth fell open. "Suspended?"

"Yeah."

"Why, for fuck's sake? He's a great student, and he's *never* been in trouble before."

"I know, I know." Bo rubbed his free hand over his forehead. "The principal said he was disrupting the class, that he refused to stop and that he threw a pencil at his teacher when she reprimanded him."

Surprised, Sam blinked. "That doesn't sound like Adrian at all."

"No, it doesn't."

Sam pulled Bo closer. "You sure you don't want me to come with you?"

"I'm sure. Thanks, though." Bo tilted his face up and pressed a swift kiss to Sam's lips. "I need to go. I'll tell you what I find out later."

"Okay." Sam squeezed Bo's hand, then let him go. "Call me if you need me."

With a wan smile, Bo nodded and turned away. Sam stood with his shoulders hunched against the cold and watched while Bo climbed into his car and backed out into the tree-lined street. Sam didn't go back inside until the car was out of sight.

∞

Bo returned half an hour later with a sullen Adrian in tow. The boy ignored Sam's greeting and stomped into his father's office in a nearly visible cloud of preteen fury. The door slammed shut behind him.

Danny glanced at the office door, then raised her eyebrows at Bo before returning to her work. Shaking his head, Bo crossed to Sam's desk and dropped into an empty chair beside him. "Don't ask."

"You got it, boss-man." David spun his chair around to face Bo. "You want me to take him out for ice cream or something?"

Bo smiled. "That's very nice of you, but there's no need. We're not staying after all. I'm taking Adrian home. He and I need to have a talk."

A sudden attack of nerves churned Sam's stomach. He never knew whether to involve himself in Bo's family affairs or not. Sean and Adrian weren't his children. However, they were part of his life now via his relationship with Bo. What he hadn't quite worked out was precisely what role he played in their lives. Trying to be a parent to them felt horribly awkward. He did the best he could, for Bo's sake, but he always felt out of his depth.

Sam licked his lips. "Do you want me to come with you, or would you rather I stayed here?"

"Would you mind coming with me?"

Damn. "Of course I don't mind."

The relief which flooded Bo's face gave Sam a guilty twinge in his gut. "Thank you, Sam. I really need your support for this."

"No problem." Forcing a smile, Sam laid a hand on Bo's knee. "Hey, why didn't the school call Janine?"

Bo's face clouded. "They did. She didn't answer her cell, so they called Lee's. He told them Janine was on assignment and he couldn't leave work, so they finally called me."

Across the room, Dean winced, the expression only half hidden by the stack of papers he'd just pulled off the printer. He didn't say anything, for which Sam was grateful. The tightness in Bo's voice announced loud and clear how he felt about Lee being called before him. No one, least of all Bo, needed it spoken out loud.

Bet I'm not even on the contact list at all, Sam thought, not without bitterness. He might not be very skilled at parenting—yet—but he cared about both boys and wanted to be available to help if needed. It stung that after all he and Bo had gone through to be together, their relationship remained unacknowledged by so many people in Sean and Adrian's lives.

Some days, he felt invisible to the world outside this office, and it hurt.

With a deep sigh, Bo rose to his feet. "Well, I suppose there's no point in putting off the inevitable. Sam, how soon can you be ready to go?"

"Depends. Is it okay if I finish this research tomorrow?"

"Yes, that'll be fine."

"Then I can leave right now, if you want."

Bo nodded. "That would be good."

Sam bookmarked the web page he'd been reviewing, then shut down the computer. He pushed out of his chair. "Okay, let's go."

"Good luck," David said, turning back to his work.

Sam let out a wry laugh. "Thanks."

While Bo went to his office to get Adrian, Dean trailed Sam to the front door. "Don't worry, Sam. You'll be fine."

Arching an eyebrow at Dean, Sam grabbed his jacket and pulled it on. "I hope you're right. I'm learning this stuff as I go. It's pretty hard sometimes."

"I bet." Dean glanced at Bo and Adrian, who had just emerged from Bo's office. "See y'all tomorrow."

Giving Dean's arm a quick squeeze, Sam followed Bo and Adrian out the front door.

They rode home in an oppressive silence, Sam at the wheel with Bo beside him and Adrian sulking in the backseat. Sam squinted through the windshield at the rain-blurred street. The drizzle had turned into a downpour in the last few minutes, cutting visibility to a few yards and transforming approaching headlights into tiny pixilated suns. It took every ounce of his concentration just to keep the car on the road.

For once, he was grateful for the intensity of the storms which tended to hit this city. If it wasn't for the distraction of driving through the deluge, the tension crackling between Bo and his son would've been enough to send Sam around the bend.

Unfortunately—to Sam's mind, at least—the two-mile trip was a short one, even with the weather slowing them down. Sam pulled into their assigned parking space and killed the engine, part of him wishing he could hide in the car during the coming confrontation between Bo and Adrian.

"There's a poncho under your seat," Bo told the boy, his voice cool. "You can wear it."

"I don't need a *poncho*," Adrian sneered. "I'm not a baby."

Bo closed his eyes. Sam watched him, worried. Maybe Adrian didn't realize how close Bo was to exploding, but Sam did. He touched Bo's knee, silently begging him to stay in control. Yelling at Adrian right now would only make things worse.

Opening his eyes, Bo gave Sam a tiny smile and a nod, then turned to fix Adrian with a stern look. "Fine. Put it over your book bag, though. You might not melt, but your books and papers will."

Silence. Adrian's anger filled the air like an electric charge, making Sam's skin itch. Seized by a sudden need to escape, he undid his seat belt, opened the car door and stepped out into the storm. The shock of cold felt good. He lifted his face, savoring the sting of the rain on his skin.

A few seconds later, Bo and Adrian climbed out of the car. Adrian's backpack formed a hump beneath the yellow poncho. The hood didn't quite cover his murderous expression.

Sam followed Bo and Adrian up the front porch steps. Bo unlocked the front door, and the three of them trudged inside. A young woman in blue sweats emerged from the nearest apartment, umbrella in hand. She gave them a nod on her way out, brown ponytail bobbing.

They didn't meet anyone else as they trudged up the stairs to their apartment. Sam knew it was just his nerves which made the silence seem so eerie—nearly all of their neighbors worked or attended school during the week, so of course the place was quiet—but knowing that didn't make him any less jumpy. He wondered if the parenting stuff would ever get any easier, or if he was fated to suffer this overwhelming sense of approaching doom every time he had to help Bo deal with discipline issues.

Inside the apartment, Sam flipped the switch to turn on the two standing lamps in the living area. Adrian tore off the poncho and threw it on the floor, then dropped his backpack beside it.

Bo took his son firmly by the shoulders and steered him to the sofa before he could stomp off to his room. "Sit," Bo ordered. "I want to talk to you."

The glare Adrian shot at his father burned with rebellion, but he did as he was told. Sam curled into the chair opposite the couch, hoping he'd be able to keep out of whatever was about to happen.

"I already told you I didn't do it," Adrian muttered.

"Yes, I know what you said." Bo sat beside Adrian, studying his face. "Son, I'd like to believe you. But according to your teacher, you were the only student sitting close enough to the bookshelf to knock those books off it. And she said she saw you throw that pencil at her."

Scowling, Adrian crossed his arms and attempted to stare a

hole in the floor. "I don't care what she *thinks* she saw. I didn't do it."

"Then who did?"

"I don't know! It just *happened,* okay?"

"Books don't go flying off a shelf all by themselves, and pencils certainly don't throw themselves at people."

In his memory, Sam saw Lee's worried face as he told them about the strange happenings at his and Janine's house—shadows, noises, objects moving by themselves. A disturbing suspicion began to take root in Sam's mind.

"Well, I guess someone else did it then, didn't they?" Adrian spat.

Bo didn't comment on the caustic tone in the child's voice. Turning sideways, he tucked one leg beneath him. "Adrian, look at me."

The boy cut his eyes sideways to meet his father's gaze with a defiant glare. Bo sighed. "We all make mistakes, son. We all do things we know are wrong. You can't change what's already happened, but you *can* take responsibility for your actions."

Adrian's jaw clenched just like Bo's did when he was angry and trying to hold it in. "I didn't do it."

Bo's dark eyes sparked with frustration. "Adrian, don't lie to me."

"I'm not lying! I *didn't do it!*"

Before Sam could wonder why the air in the room suddenly felt so heavy, the bulb in the lamp beside him exploded with a pop. Shards of glass pinged against the wooden floor.

Adrian leaped to his feet, his face stricken. "*Now* look what you made me do!" Without waiting for an answer, he ran into his and Sean's bedroom and slammed the door behind him.

A stunned silence fell. Sam stared at the lamp for a

moment, then turned to look at Bo. The color had leeched from Bo's face. His gaze caught Sam's, and Sam knew they were thinking the same thing.

Maybe Lee and the boys weren't imagining things after all.

Chapter Six

Since Adrian refused to come out of his room, Bo went in. Adrian protested, but as the door had no lock he didn't have much choice in the matter.

Sam busied himself cleaning up the broken glass and changing the bulb in the lamp. Bo had left the bedroom door open, and Sam tried not to listen to Bo's increasingly ragged pleas for Adrian to talk to him. Hearing Bo's control erode under his son's obstinate silence made Sam's heart ache.

By the time Bo gave up and left Adrian alone, Sam had swept the kitchen and living room and washed the dishes, and was starting to wonder how in the hell he was supposed to keep himself occupied if Bo stayed in there any longer. His relief at seeing Bo emerge from the bedroom evaporated when he caught sight of Bo's expression. He looked frightened and defeated.

Hurrying forward, Sam gathered Bo into his arms and held him tight. Bo clung to him, face buried in his neck and both fists clenched in the back of his shirt. "What happened?" Sam murmured, stroking Bo's hair. "Is he okay? Are *you* okay?"

"I don't know, Sam. I just don't know." Bo lifted his head to meet Sam's gaze. "He won't talk to me. I think he might be psychokinetic like you, and I know you're thinking the same. But how in the hell am I supposed to figure it out if he won't *tell* me anything?"

Sam stroked his thumb across Bo's forehead, trying to smooth the worried crease from between his eyes. "Do you want me to try talking to him? I mean, I know he doesn't like me, but maybe in this case he'll be willing to talk to me since I've experienced similar things."

Hope lit Bo's eyes. "That's true. Would you try?"

"Of course I will," Sam promised, ignoring the way his stomach lurched at the thought. "If he really is having latent psychokinesis emerge, I'll do anything I can to help him deal with it."

Letting go of Sam's shirt, Bo cradled Sam's face in both hands and leaned their foreheads together. "Thank you, Sam," he whispered. "I love you so much."

Sam's throat went tight. Tilting his head, he planted a tender kiss on Bo's mouth. "I love you too."

He felt Bo's lips curve into a smile. They kissed again, a little longer this time, a little deeper, and Sam wished they were alone. He shoved the thought away. Now wasn't the time.

When the kiss broke, Sam reluctantly drew out of Bo's embrace. "I'll go try to talk to Adrian now. Wish me luck."

"Good luck." Bo gave Sam's hand a squeeze before letting go.

Squaring his shoulders, Sam paced across the floor and down the short hallway to the boys' room. The door hung halfway open. Sam rapped his knuckles against the wood. "Adrian? Can I come in?"

Silence. "Whatever," Adrian mumbled a couple of endless seconds later.

Sam shot a swift glance back at Bo, who gave him an encouraging smile. Hoping he wasn't about to fuck things up beyond repair, Sam pushed the door open and walked inside.

Adrian lay curled on his bed, both hands tucked beneath his chin. He looked even younger than he was, small and scared and vulnerable, and Sam's heart went out to him. As difficult as the boy could be at times, he was only a child. An eleven-year-old, trying to cope with an ability which would be overwhelming for someone three times his age.

Sam perched on the end of Adrian's bed, wondering how to start. Obviously, Adrian himself believed he'd made the light bulb explode. He hadn't seemed surprised, either, which made Sam think the boy already knew he might be causing some—if not all—of the strange events at Lee and Janine's house.

The direct approach worked before. It seems to be the best way to reach him.

Sam cleared his throat. "So. What makes you think you caused the light bulb to explode?"

Adrian shot him a look full of unspoken resentment. "*You* know. You can do it too." The simple statement told Sam all he needed to know about what Adrian had experienced lately.

Seeing no point in denying the obvious, Sam nodded. "Yes, I can. Of course I didn't know it when I was your age. My talents started coming out a little later, and I had no idea what was really going on until last year. I always thought I was just...weird, you know? A freak."

Adrian was watching Sam now, dark eyes curious. Encouraged, Sam plowed on. "When I found out the strange things that had been happening to me were real, and were caused by an ability called psychokinesis, I didn't know what to think. It was a relief, in a way, because it made me feel like less of a freak to know it had a real cause. But it was scary too, because I didn't know how to control it, and I didn't want my abilities to cause anyone I loved to get hurt."

"Like my dad."

73

Surprised, Sam nodded. "Yeah. Like your dad. And my friends at BCPI."

Sitting up, Adrian drew his knees to his chin and wrapped both arms around his legs. His expression was blank, but fear glittered in his eyes. "I don't want my mom to get hurt," he whispered, so softly Sam almost didn't hear him. "Or Sean. Or my dad."

Sam didn't mention Lee's absence in the list, or his own. "I won't lie to you, Adrian. There's always the possibility of people around you being hurt. Most of the time that doesn't happen, though. It can be very frightening when you hear noises, or things move or break, and you know you caused it without meaning to. But the likelihood that anyone'll get hurt is low. And chances are, when you get older it'll all just go away." He didn't mention the possibility of Adrian's new ability causing one of the interdimensional portals to open. The boy was obviously frightened enough without adding to it. Sam figured he and Bo would have to discuss what to tell Adrian about the portals.

Adrian looked at the wall. "What if it doesn't go away?"

What indeed? Sam's pulse raced. He knew what he had to do—what he *wanted* to do—but God, it was a terrifying responsibility.

"I can help you learn to control it," Sam heard himself offer. "I learned. I can control my ability pretty well now. I can teach you, if you'll let me."

Adrian's gaze snapped back to study Sam's face with a shrewdness far beyond his years. Sam waited as calmly as he could. It galled him to feel so intimidated by an eleven-year-old. But he figured all step-parents—*is that what I am?*—felt that way from time to time, and Adrian was hardly an average child. Plus it wasn't every day that a guy was faced with the prospect of teaching his lover's son to control his psychokinetic powers.

Just when Sam thought he couldn't stand the silence any longer, Adrian turned away and lay down again, curling on his side. "Maybe."

Sam watched the boy, trying to think of the best way to proceed. He had to tread carefully here. Agreeing to even the possibility of Sam helping him was a huge step for Adrian. Sam didn't want to do or say anything to scare him off.

"Okay," Sam said. "Why don't I let you think it over, huh? And you can tell me what you decide to do."

Adrian didn't answer, but Sam knew he'd heard. Pushing to his feet, Sam left the room and shut the door.

He found Bo in the kitchen, stirring milk into a cup of peppermint tea. Bo looked up when Sam walked in. "Well?"

Sam smiled at the mingled hope and apprehension in Bo's eyes. "He didn't say much, but it was enough. He believes he's responsible for what's been happening at his mom's house, and I think he'd like to learn to control it."

Bo's eyebrows rose. "You think?"

"Well, he said he didn't want you or the rest of his family to get hurt because of what he can do. I offered to teach him how to control it. He didn't accept, but he didn't tell me no either." Sam shrugged. "I think he might be willing to let me help him."

"God, that would be fantastic." Smiling, Bo reached out and pulled Sam into his arms. "I know how hard it must've been for you to do that, Sam. To talk with Adrian, and offer to help him."

"Only because I'm still getting used to being...well, whatever I am to the boys." Draping both arms over Bo's shoulders, Sam kissed his brow. "I just hope I can actually help him."

"So do I." Pressing closer, Bo rubbed his cheek against

Sam's. "The EMF at Janine and Lee's house is high, even without the entertainment center leakage factored in. If Adrian really does have psychokinetic powers..."

He didn't finish the thought, but he didn't need to. They both knew what the combination of high EMF and uncontrolled psychokinesis could do.

Don't forget what's happened to most other people who can open the portals.

A chill ran up Sam's spine. In the very few portal cases he'd managed to dig up in his research, he'd only found one person besides himself who'd acted as a focus to open a portal and not ended up catatonic. Josephine Royce, who had opened a portal at Oleander House decades ago and lost her lover to the things on the other side. Her last words, scrawled on a sheet of paper stuck in a forgotten magazine, proclaimed her intention of following her love into the void. She was never heard from again, leaving Sam as the only living person able to open an interdimensional gateway and survive with his mind intact.

The thing was, he still had no idea *why* he wasn't currently a drooling vegetable in a nursing home somewhere. The thought of Adrian suffering that fate was unbearable. Knowing that Bo was thinking the same thing hurt Sam's heart.

"Maybe we're getting ahead of ourselves," Sam said, stroking Bo's hair. "I mean, I'm pretty sure he's psychokinetic. But that doesn't have to mean anything will ever happen other than the usual poltergeist-type activity."

"I know." Bo let out a shaky breath. "At least he's safe for the moment. At least we have a few hours to think. Maybe we can come up with some sort of plan before Janine finds out Adrian's here and comes after him."

"That's right." Sam nuzzled Bo's ear. "Don't worry. We'll figure it out. We'll make sure nothing happens to the boys, or anyone else."

Bo nodded, his head coming to rest on Sam's shoulder, but the tension in his body remained. Not that Sam blamed him. Sam didn't entirely believe himself either.

∞

At four o'clock, Lee showed up with Sean in tow to retrieve Adrian. Bo barely got the door open before Sean threw himself at his father so hard Bo grunted. "Hi, Dad."

"Hi, son." Smiling, Bo ruffled Sean's hair. "How was school?"

Sean scrunched up his face. "Boring. Adrian's lucky he got to leave early."

"Not really. He's in trouble." Bo stopped Sean's inevitable questions with a raised hand. "Not right now. I'll explain it all later."

"'Kay." Letting go of his dad, Sean crossed to the sofa and threw his book bag on it. "Where's Adrian?"

"In your bedroom," Sam answered. "Bo, you want me to get him, or should he and Sean stay in their room for this?"

Lee frowned, looking puzzled. "For what?"

Pulling his braid over his shoulder, Bo tugged on the tail. "Lee, we need to talk. Do you have a minute?"

Lee's gaze darted from Bo to Sam and back again. "Oh. Yes, of course."

"Good." Bo turned to his youngest son, who had plopped onto the couch and was reaching for the TV remote. "Sean, I need you to go to your bedroom, okay? You and Adrian can watch TV in there."

"All right." Leaping to his feet, Sean raced for the bedroom and flung the door open. Adrian's indignant protest floated from the room.

Lee waited until Sean had shut the door again before speaking up. "Okay. What did you want to talk about?"

Moving closer to Sam, Bo took his hand. "When will Janine be home?"

"Late tonight. I'm not sure exactly what time." Lee frowned. "What's going on? I know Adrian's been suspended, and trust me, Janine will discipline him for it. Is there something else happening that we should know about?"

The muscle in Bo's jaw tightened and relaxed. "Sam and I have both spoken with Adrian, and we believe the incident at the school is a bit more complex than it appears on the surface."

Lee shook his head. "I'm sorry, I don't understand."

Bo glanced at Sam, who gave his hand an encouraging squeeze. They'd spent a couple of hours that afternoon talking about what to do before confronting Adrian with their decision. Surprisingly, Adrian had accepted it without argument. Sam thought he'd seen relief in Adrian's eyes.

"It's kind of complicated," Bo began. "But we believe it might not be safe for Adrian to go back to your place right now. I'd like for him to stay here for a little while. Sean can stay as well, if he'd like to."

"What do you mean, not safe? Janine would never do anything to hurt either of those boys, and neither would I."

"I know. That's not exactly what I meant."

Lee's eyes went wide. "My God, Bo, are you suggesting Adrian is *dangerous*?"

"No. Well, not exactly." Sighing, Bo rubbed his eyes with

the hand not clutched tight around Sam's. "Okay, here's the thing. We believe Adrian may be developing an ability called psychokinesis. That means—"

"I know what it is," Lee interrupted, his face white. "How do you know that? Have you tested him?"

"We haven't, no, but earlier today when he was angry one of our light bulbs broke for no reason. He also claims that he didn't cause the trouble he was accused of causing in class, and after what we saw this afternoon I believe him." Bo glanced at Sam, as if looking for the right way to explain it. "The signs point to psychokinesis, Lee. What you've been experiencing at your house sounds like a classic case of poltergeist activity. And the most widely accepted theory—the one which has proven to be the case many times in the past—is that poltergeist activity is actually caused by latent psychokinesis, often in a teen or preteen experiencing uncontrolled, strongly negative emotions."

"Yes, I've heard of Fodor's Theory." Lee twisted his hands together, an odd mix of curiosity and horror on his face. "You think this might be what's happening at our house? And that Adrian is the cause of it?"

Bo nodded. "Exactly."

"All right, I can see that." A frown creased Lee's brow. "But I don't understand why that would put anyone in danger. From what I've read on the subject, situations like this are usually frightening, but not physically dangerous. The worst thing that's happened so far at our house was me being scratched, and even that wasn't terrible."

"Normally it wouldn't be dangerous, no, but..." Bo's fingers clenched and relaxed around Sam's. "How much do you know about the interdimensional portals BCPI has been dealing with in the past year?"

Lee shrugged. "Not as much as I'd like to. It's a fascinating topic."

"So far, every portal we've dealt with has been in an area of elevated EMF," Sam explained, rubbing his thumb along the back of Bo's hand. "We've also discovered that people with psychokinesis can sometimes act as a focus of sorts for the portal to open, as long as conditions are right. It's happened to me, actually."

"Conditions such as a high EMF level." Lee's gaze darted back and forth between Sam and Bo. "The electrician's coming back tomorrow to do some rewiring and such in the living room. He said he can fix the electromagnetism leak there."

Sam nodded, impressed with how quickly Lee had put two and two together. "That's good. But the baseline EMF in your house is still on the high side. Not dangerous in and of itself, but combined with uncontrolled psychokinesis it could mean the possibility of a portal opening."

"Oh. I see." Lee stumbled over to the counter and leaned against it, his expression stunned. "Do you really think that could happen?"

Bo shifted his weight so that his shoulder pressed to Sam's. "We hope it won't. Like you said, it hasn't happened yet, and of course we know so little about the portals overall that it's hard to say what—if any—other conditions need to be in place for them to open. But I'd much rather err on the side of caution when it comes to the boys' safety."

"Yes, I can understand that."

Lee sounded thoroughly shaken. Not that Sam blamed him. The light-bulb incident made Sam a bit nervous about having Adrian around, and he knew there would be no portals opening here.

"Good," Bo said, sounding relieved. "I know Janine's going to be angry that the boys are staying here. I'll call her later, and you and she can come by the office tomorrow. I'll explain the whole thing to her, and she can yell at me if she wants."

Lee shook his head. "Bo, I'm sorry, but I can't let the boys stay here. You know how Janine feels about you having them when it's not your time."

"I understand that," Bo answered, his words clipped and careful. "And I wouldn't ask if I didn't feel it was necessary."

Lee eyed Bo with transparent caution. "I know. And if I thought there was compelling evidence to suggest the kids really were in danger, I'd agree with you. But you said yourself you don't know if the portal really could open. I'm sorry, but no. I'm going to have to take the boys home with me."

An angry flush climbed up Bo's neck and crept into his cheeks. Sam let go of Bo's hand and slipped an arm around his shoulders instead. Bo losing his temper wouldn't help their case any.

"It's okay, Sam." Shaking off Sam's arm, Bo took a step toward Lee. "I know you're afraid of what Janine is going to say, or do. Believe me, I'm not looking forward to facing her either. But I'm afraid I'm going to have to put my foot down. The boys are staying here, at least for tonight, and we'll talk over the situation tomorrow."

Lee gaped. "You can't do that."

"I can, and I am."

"We have custody."

Sam winced. Of all the things Lee could've said, that was probably the worst.

"*Janine* has custody," Bo growled, dark eyes snapping with fury. "You do *not*. Right now, *my* children are in danger, and I will do whatever it takes to protect them." Brushing past Lee, Bo flung open the door. "Go home. Bring Janine to the office tomorrow and we'll talk."

Lee backed out the door, his expression sorrowful. "I wish you wouldn't do this, Bo."

"I wish I didn't have to." Bo shut the door on Lee's stunned expression and covered his face with his hands. "Shit."

"You can say that again." Sam closed the distance between them and wrapped his arms around Bo from behind. "For what it's worth, I think you did the right thing."

"I know. I had no choice, really." Turning in Sam's embrace, Bo slipped his arms around Sam's waist and rested his head in the curve of Sam's neck. "Janine's going to be furious."

"Yes, she is." Sam rubbed his cheek against Bo's silky hair.

"But at least the boys are safe, for now."

"Yeah. And that's the most important thing."

Silence fell. The crackle of alien laser guns drifted from Sean and Adrian's bedroom, followed by an angry wail from Sean and a victorious whoop from Adrian. Sam smiled.

"She could press charges for this," Bo whispered, his breath warm against Sam's throat. "She could keep me from ever seeing them again."

Sam's stomach knotted. "I don't think even Janine could be that awful. As horrible as she is to us most of the time, she does love Sean and Adrian. She knows how important you are to them. She wouldn't take you away from them."

"I'd like to think you're right. But she'd be within her legal rights to have me arrested." Bo lifted his head and stared at Sam with dread in his eyes. "Lee can't have gotten far. Maybe we should go after him and let him take the boys back with him."

Cupping Bo's face in his hands, Sam held Bo's gaze with a

calm he didn't feel. "Whatever you want to do, Bo, I'm with you. Okay?"

Bo stood there gnawing his bottom lip, clutching Sam's ribs in a death grip. Sam kept quiet and waited. If Adrian truly had psychokinetic powers—and Sam's gut said he did—the possibility of him accidentally opening an interdimensional portal at Lee and Janine's house was one they couldn't ignore. Which was why they'd decided to try and keep the boys with them for the time being. However, nothing had happened so far which would suggest anything other than standard poltergeist-type activity unwittingly caused by a troubled preteen with emerging psychokinetic abilities. If Bo thought keeping the kids out of that house wasn't worth the risk of losing his parental rights, Sam saw no reason to try to change his mind.

After a couple of indecisive minutes, Bo shook his head. "No. Their safety is more important. We'll keep them here."

"Okay." Sam caressed Bo's cheeks with his thumbs. "It'll be all right, Bo. You'll see."

Bo didn't answer. Instead, he pulled Sam's body flush against his own. His heartbeat galloped against Sam's chest. Sliding both arms snug around Bo's waist, Sam held him tight.

∞

In Sam's nightmare, something chased him through cramped, dark hallways. He ran, not daring to look back for fear of what he might see. The unseen menace shook the floor as it pounded after him. Its icy breath froze the flesh at the nape of his neck.

Something warm moved against his bare skin. "Sam, wake up," a voice murmured in his ear.

Shaking off the dream with a sense of relief, Sam opened his eyes. The room was dark. A faint glow from the streetlight outside leaked in around the edge of the curtains.

The thumping noise sounded again. A jolt of pure terror shot up Sam's spine before he realized it was someone knocking on the door.

Glancing at the clock, Sam groaned. "What the fuck? Who the hell's trying to knock our door down at five thirty in the damn morning?"

"I'm betting it's Janine." Bo switched on the bedside lamp, slipped out of Sam's arms and climbed out of bed. "I'll go see. You can stay here."

"No way. I'm coming with you."

Bo gave Sam a half-irritated, half-affectionate look as he threw the covers back and got up. "It'll just set her off if she sees you."

"Tough. I live here. If she doesn't want to see me, she shouldn't come banging on our door before dawn."

Sighing, Bo opened the bedroom door and stalked out into the hall with Sam at his heels. The knocking sounded again, pounding so hard the door shook. The impatient chime of the doorbell followed.

"Goddammit, she's going to wake the whole building." Bo flipped open the deadbolt, undid the chain and flung the door open. "Janine, what the hell—"

"Shut up." Shoving Bo aside, Janine stormed into the room, walked straight up to Sam and dealt a stinging slap across his face. "You. Stay *the fuck* away from my kids."

Chapter Seven

Sam gaped at her, speechless. Her cheeks were fiery red, her eyes blazing. Fine tremors shook her from head to toe.

He laid a hand over the palm-shaped warmth on his cheek. "Good morning to you too. Reasonable and pleasant as ever, I see."

She drew herself up, obviously preparing a scathing retort. Or possibly another slap. Sam stared straight at her, daring her to do it again.

Before either of them could escalate things, Bo stepped between the two of them, one hand held palm-out toward Janine. "All right. Both of you just calm down. Janine, Sam had nothing to do with this. It was my idea to keep the boys here last night."

She shifted her death glare from Sam to Bo. "Yes, I'm sure your little fucktoy's made you believe it was your idea."

Before Sam could decide if he should speak up or if it would just cause more problems, Bo jumped to his defense. "I don't care how angry you are with me, you do *not* come to *my* home and insult Sam like that. As I said before, he had nothing—*nothing*—to do with it. I am Sean and Adrian's father, and I made the decision to keep them here because I believe having Adrian at your house endangers *everyone* there. Frankly, I couldn't care less right now what happens to you, but

I absolutely will not put my boys in danger. Period."

"Oh yes, Lee told me about your little theory. God, Sam has you twisted right around his little finger, doesn't he? Now he's even got you believing our son's some kind of freak." Janine's mouth twisted into a bitter parody of a smile. "I hope the sex is worth it."

Sam bit the insides of his cheeks to keep himself from telling her exactly how good the sex was. Gloating wouldn't help the situation.

"Our sex life is none of your business." Crossing his arms, Bo leaned back against Sam, who wound an arm around his chest. "Now. Why don't you tell us why you're here?"

Janine stared at Sam's arm around Bo. An almost sorrowful expression fleeted through her eyes and was gone before Sam could grasp it. She sneered at them. "I'm here to get Sean and Adrian, of course. I thought that would be obvious."

Bo went tense, though he must've known all along that was why she'd come here. "Don't."

"You can't stop me, Bo. I have custody."

"I know, but..." Bo shook his head. His shoulders were rigid with the anger and desperation Sam knew he felt. "It isn't safe. I know you don't believe me, but you have to understand I'm only thinking of the boys."

Janine shut her eyes. She looked tired and worried. For the first time ever, Sam felt a pang of real empathy for her. If only she could meet them halfway, accept that he and Bo just wanted to keep the boys safe, they could work out the rest.

Her eyes opened. For a second, they stared straight into Sam's. He held her gaze, wishing he could bring himself to make some sort of overture of friendship, or at least compromise. But his cheek still burned, and his pride wouldn't let him do anything more than keep his insults to himself.

"Look, Bo, I know you think you're doing the right thing. That's the only reason I'm not pressing charges." Janine turned a hard gaze to Bo. "But I'm taking the boys with me. If you try to stop me, I'll have to call the police."

Bo drew a deep, shaking breath. One hand crept up to clasp Sam's where it rested on his shoulder. "Take them to Rita's, then. Or to Lee's sister, she lives in town, right? Just don't take them to your house. Please. It isn't safe."

Her mouth thinned into a stubborn line. "I think I can decide for myself what is and isn't safe for my children. Now are you going to get them, or should I do it?"

Pushing Sam's arm off, Bo took a step toward Janine. "Fine. But just remember, I'm not the one who's been trying to sabotage your relationship with our sons all these months. I'm not the one who's deliberately tried to keep you away from them every chance I got. I have to wonder what a judge would say about all the times you've tried to take the boys when it's my weekend."

A grimacing smile twisted Janine's lips. "I wonder what a judge would say about a parent whose lover tries to convince his child that he has some sort of supernatural power. Wonder whose visitation might be taken away in that scenario?"

The threat was clear. Sam couldn't see Bo's face, but he could practically smell the raw fury pouring from the other man. Bo's hands clenched into fists at his side. For one terrible second, Sam thought Bo was going to punch Janine in the face. When he turned away and stalked off toward the boys' room instead, Sam breathed a silent sigh of relief. He wondered if Janine had any idea how close she'd just come to getting a black eye.

"He's upset for no reason. The kids will be fine."

Sam turned toward Janine, keeping his expression

carefully neutral. "They'd better be."

Her lips tightened. "Believe it or not, I want to keep my children safe just as much as Bo does."

Sure you do. Bitch.

He didn't say it. Name-calling couldn't possibly help matters.

Forcing back the part of him which wanted to verbally cut Janine to ribbons, Sam took a deep breath and tried to explain his point of view rationally. "I don't doubt you have their best interest at heart, and neither does Bo. But they won't be safe if you take them back to your house. None of you will be, not as long as Adrian's there. Not until he learns to control what he can do."

"My son is *not* a freak."

"No, he's not. What he is, is a kid who has an ability he has no idea how to cope with." Sam glanced toward the hallway, where Sean's sleepy voice protested getting up so early, then turned back to Janine. "I can help him. I can teach him to control his gifts. Please let me do that."

She let out a harsh laugh, and Sam knew he hadn't gotten through to her. He hadn't expected to, really, but nothing ventured nothing gained, as the saying went.

"We both know you have nothing of value to offer my child." She glared up at him, her knuckles white where she clutched the strap of her purse. "I can't do anything about you being with Bo. But if I ever hear about you putting these ridiculous ideas into Adrian's head, I *will* call my lawyer and have Bo's visitation revoked. Am I clear?"

Sam gave her a cold smile which he knew did nothing to hide the pure loathing in his eyes. "Crystal."

"Good." She turned, a genuine smile lighting her face as Bo

emerged into the living room with both boys dragging half-asleep behind him. "Hey, sweeties. I'm sorry to have to wake you so early, but Mommy's got to get to work early. Rita's going to come pick you both up at my office and take you to school when it's time."

"I can't go to school," Adrian said, sounding exactly like his father when he was annoyed and trying not to show it. "I'm suspended."

Janine gave him a stern look. "I know. And believe me, we are going to talk about that. You'll just have to stay at work with me today. I'm sure you have schoolwork you could be doing."

Adrian scowled, but didn't answer.

Yawning, Sean rubbed his eyes. "Mom, can we go get pancakes?"

Janine glanced at her watch. "I'm sorry, honey, we don't have time."

"But I'm hungry." Sean shuffled over and grabbed his mother's jacket in both small hands. He gazed up at her with his best pleading expression. "We could eat here. I bet Dad would make pancakes."

Shaking her head, Janine rubbed the bridge of her nose. "We'll go through the drive-through at McDonald's, okay? You can get pancakes there. Now get your book bag and let's go, I have a lot to do this morning."

Bo ran gentle fingers through Sean's tousled hair. "Come on, son. Let's get your stuff together, huh?"

While Sean whined and Janine fussed at him, Sam wandered over and laid a hand on Adrian's shoulder. "The key is to control your emotions," Sam murmured, for Adrian's ears only. "If you feel yourself getting angry or frustrated and losing control, just close your eyes and take a few deep breaths.

Concentrate on something calm and happy."

Adrian glanced up at him, dark eyes wide and fearful. "What if that doesn't work?"

"Leave the room if you need to. Go outside, throw a ball around, run in circles, whatever it takes to feel calm again." Sam gave him an encouraging smile. "We'll talk more when y'all come over for your weekend, but for now this should help."

Adrian nodded and shrugged off Sam's hand just as Janine glanced over. Her eyes narrowed. "Adrian, say goodbye to your dad and let's go."

Sam watched as Sean and Adrian hugged Bo goodbye and shouldered their backpacks. Sean ran to collect a hug from Sam too, then the boys followed their mother out the door.

As soon as they'd gone, Sam went to Bo and pulled him close. Bo's body practically vibrated with rage. "They'll be all right." Sam kissed Bo's ear, hoping like hell he wasn't lying.

"They'd better be, or I'll kill Janine with my bare hands." Pulling out of Sam's arms, Bo started pacing the floor in long, fast strides. "God, I'm so *fucking* angry right now. Why couldn't she at least take them somewhere else?"

"I don't know."

"I hate that I can't do anything." Bo gave his braid a vicious yank. "What if something happens to Sean and Adrian, Sam? What if—"

"Bo. Stop." Crossing to Bo, Sam grabbed his shoulders and kissed the worried crease between his eyes. "Let's just stay calm, and try to think of how we can help Adrian without getting arrested or having your weekends taken away, okay?"

Sighing, Bo leaned against Sam's chest. "Yes. Okay. So what do you suggest?"

"Well for starters, while you were getting their stuff together and Janine was talking to Sean, I talked to Adrian for a second. I told him he needed to keep control of his temper, and gave him a couple of pointers for doing that."

"Did he listen?"

"Yeah, he did."

"Good." Bo's arms went around Sam's neck. "We'll just have to hope that helps."

"I think it will." Tilting his head, Sam brushed a light kiss across Bo's lips. "The next time the boys are here for the weekend, I'm going to start teaching Adrian how to control his abilities. We'll have to keep it secret from Janine, but I honestly don't know what else to do. He has to learn, or he'll be putting himself and everyone else in danger as long as he's in that house."

Bo stared at him, dark eyes blazing. Just as Sam was about to ask Bo if he was all right, he dove forward and took Sam's mouth in a rough, hungry kiss.

The sudden switch from angry, worried parent to equally angry, demanding lover paralyzed Sam for a moment. He recovered quickly, however, snaking an arm around Bo's waist and cupping the back of Bo's head in the opposite hand. Usually, confrontations like the one they'd just had with Janine sent Bo into a brooding silence. Every now and then, though, his wrath found its outlet in sex. Apparently this was one of those times.

That was fine with Sam. He liked being able to help Bo work through his frustration, for more reasons than one.

By the time the kiss broke, Sam was hard as granite and Bo's erection dug into Sam's hip. Without a word, Bo took Sam's hand and dragged him to their bedroom. Inside, he pushed Sam onto the bed and fell on top of him. Sam grunted as Bo's weight landed on his stomach.

Pushing up on one elbow, Bo shoved a hand down the front of Sam's thin sleep pants and curled his fingers around Sam's shaft. Sam moaned.

Bo leaned down until his lips brushed Sam's. "I want to fuck you."

The growl in Bo's voice raised the hairs on Sam's arms. He shuddered as Bo's thumb caught the sensitive tip of his cock. Angling his head, he arched up to capture Bo's lips with his. Bo's mouth opened, his tongue shoving in to tangle with Sam's. Groaning, Sam clutched at Bo's shoulders. His head whirled. God, he loved Bo's aggressive side.

Bo pushed away before Sam could come from rutting into his hand. Sliding off the edge of the bed, Bo stood and peeled out of his pajama pants and long-sleeved T-shirt while Sam squirmed out of his own clothes. Sam's head was still stuck inside his shirt when Bo shoved his legs apart and wedged himself between them. Teeth dug into the juncture of Sam's neck and shoulder, Bo's slick finger breached his entrance, and Sam let out a low whimper.

Finally freeing himself from his shirt, Sam threw the garment on the floor and pulled his knees up to his chest. "Bo. Do it."

Bo's breath hitched against Sam's neck. Sitting back on his heels, Bo opened the lube he'd evidently retrieved from the bedside drawer, slicked his cock and tossed the bottle aside. It thudded onto the throw rug beside the bed. His gaze locked with Sam's, Bo lined up the head of his prick with Sam's hole and impaled him with one hard thrust.

It stung, but only for a second. By the time Bo dropped forward onto his hands and started pounding into Sam's ass, the burn was gone, swallowed up in a pleasure so huge Sam's vision swam with the intensity of it. Bracing his heels on the small of Bo's back, Sam dug his fingers into Bo's buttocks and hung on. The firm muscles flexed beneath his palms, driving Bo into him hard enough to make his skull vibrate.

Sam grinned with his face pressed into Bo's neck. He treasured the times when he and Bo made love soft and slow, with gentle touches and tender kisses. But he *lived* for moments like this, with Bo's breath harsh in his ear and Bo's cock fucking him so hard he forgot his own name.

Bliss. Pure, brain-melting bliss.

Before long, needy little sounds began to bleed from Bo's throat. His rhythm faltered, his thrusts becoming shorter and sharper. Through the red haze in his brain, Sam recognized the signs of Bo's approaching climax. Reaching up, Sam buried a hand in Bo's hair and angled his face for a rough, graceless kiss.

"Come on," Sam panted into Bo's mouth. "Come inside me."

A violent tremor ran through Bo's body. "Sam, oh God."

Bo's cock jerked, his hips pumping as he came deep in Sam's ass. The movement nudged Sam's gland, sending him tumbling into orgasm right behind Bo.

Letting his legs fall to the mattress, Sam wrapped both arms around Bo and pulled him down into a tight embrace. Bo's prick slipped from Sam's body with the motion. Sam yipped, and Bo laughed. It was a nice sound to hear.

Sam kissed Bo's smiling mouth. "Feel better now?"

"You know I do." Bo settled against Sam's chest, his head tucked into the curve of Sam's neck. "Thank you."

Chuckling, Sam kissed Bo's hair. "Don't thank me. It's not like I didn't get anything out of it."

"Mm. True." Bo's arm snaked around Sam's middle. He kissed Sam's throat. "I love you."

Sam smiled. "I love you too."

They fell silent. Bo slung a leg across Sam's thighs and cuddled closer. Sam drifted into a half doze, one hand tracing lazily up and down Bo's bare back.

Bo's soft voice nudged Sam out of his torpor. "What do we do now?"

Sam knew Bo wasn't talking about plans for the morning. He hugged Bo tighter against his side. "I guess we wait for our next weekend with the boys, and hope for the best in the meantime."

"I guess you're right." Bo's thumb rubbed tiny circles around Sam's right nipple. "I hate feeling this helpless. Even if the kids were here with us, I still couldn't do anything to help Adrian deal with what he's going through. I hate that."

"I'm sorry, Bo. I wish I could do more to help."

Bo lifted his head to gaze into Sam's eyes. "Sam, you've already offered to teach him how to control his psychokinesis. That's something I could never give him, no matter how much I might want to." He shifted enough to lay a hand on Sam's cheek. "Don't ever think you don't do enough. You've done more than I ever could've asked you to."

The expression in Bo's eyes brought a hot flush to Sam's cheeks. Not knowing what to say, he opted to pull Bo's face down and kiss him. Bo opened up with the soft sigh which always made Sam's heart lurch. A wave of tingling warmth spread through Sam's body when Bo's tongue slid against his.

Closing his eyes, Sam let the sensation carry him away. There'd be plenty of time for worry later.

Chapter Eight

The next few days passed without a word from Janine, Lee or either of the children. Bo was nearly beside himself with worry, convinced the lack of communication meant something had gone horribly wrong and Janine was trying to keep the truth from him.

For his own part, Sam didn't know what to believe. He was concerned about the boys, but he couldn't help feeling that Lee, at least, would contact them if anything bad happened.

Not that he'd had any luck convincing Bo of that. By Halloween, Bo was on the verge of snatching the children from Lee and Janine's house and making a run for it.

"I'll go over there tonight," Bo said, standing at his office window and staring out into the bright afternoon. "Janine'll be taking the boys out trick-or-treating around six thirty, I can catch them on their way out."

Shaking his head, Sam crossed from the bookcase he'd been perusing to stand beside Bo. "I don't think that's a good idea."

"I just want to check on them."

"Yes, I know. But Janine might not see it that way."

"I won't make trouble." Bo turned and pinned Sam with a sorrowful look. "It's been four days since she took them. I'm worried, Sam. Why haven't we heard from them?"

Sam slid his arm around Bo's waist. "We usually don't hear from them between visits. Maybe it just means everything's been quiet."

Bo didn't say anything, but some of the fear faded from his eyes. Sam was glad. He hated seeing Bo eaten up with anxiety as he'd been the past four days.

A knock sounded, followed by the office door flying open. "Oh. Oops, sorry. Didn't realize y'all were, um, busy."

Dean's tone wasn't nearly as apologetic as his words. Letting go of Bo, Sam turned to meet Dean's sparkling eyes and wide, teasing grin. "Don't you know by now not to just walk in here when the door's closed?"

"Hey, I'm not David, you know. I'm just waiting for the day when I actually catch y'all going at it."

Bo pivoted to face Dean. "Okay, Dean, what did you—?" He stopped mid-sentence and stared. "What the hell are you wearing?"

"A costume." Dean glanced down at the solid black unitard clinging to his body like a second skin. "You said we could."

"Yes, but..." Bo gestured helplessly at Dean. "I didn't really expect anyone to come to work dressed as a cat."

Dean reached up to run a thumb along the edge of one of the black and white pointed ears perched on top of his head. "But I look so *hot* in this."

The corner of Bo's mouth twitched. "Relax, Dean, you can keep the costume on. I was just surprised, that's all. Unlike some people." He shot a pointed look at Sam.

Sam shrugged. "I saw it earlier. You were already holed up in here when Dean got here this morning."

"Hm. You're right." Moving away from Sam's side, Bo

dropped into the chair behind his desk. "So, Dean, what was it you needed? Or were you really just hoping to catch Sam and me with our pants down? So to speak."

Sam laughed out loud, some of his worry for Bo falling away with Bo's light words. If Bo was making jokes, he must be feeling better about things, which was good.

Dean's grin disappeared, replaced by a sudden nervousness. "Um. Well, Janine called, she said—"

"Wait, Janine called?" Bo leaned forward, frowning. "Why didn't you put her through?"

"She didn't give me a chance. Danny would've done it anyway, but she was in the bathroom, and you know I'm not as good as she is at doing phone stuff." Dean fiddled with the ribbon around his waist holding his tail on. "So anyway, Janine said tell you she's bringing the boys over here after school."

Sam's heart gave a funny lurch. He didn't know whether to be relieved or alarmed.

From the expression on Bo's face, he felt the same. "Did she say why?"

"No. She said she'd explain when they got here." Dean bit his lip. "Sorry, Bo. I wish I could tell you more. Is there anything I can do?"

Bo shook his head, a forced smile on his face. "No, I'm fine. I guess we'll just have to wait and see what Janine has to say."

Nodding, Dean backed out the door. "Okay. We'll let you know when they get here."

"All right, thanks." Bo waited until Dean had left and shut the door before dropping his head into his hands. "Christ, Sam. What the fuck? Is Janine *trying* to drive me crazy?"

"I wouldn't put it past her." Moving behind Bo's chair, Sam laid his hands on Bo's shoulders and started kneading the tight muscles. "Seriously, that's probably it. She's just holding out on you to make you worry, because she can. I'm sure there's nothing wrong." He kept his doubts to himself. Bo didn't need to hear that right now.

"God, I hope you're right." Bo tilted his head back, resting it against Sam's belly, and smiled up at him. "Thanks for trying to make me feel better. Even if neither of us believes what you just said."

"Damn. You can see right through me, can't you?"

"I've had lots of practice." Bo reached a hand toward Sam. "Kiss me."

Sam was more than happy to obey. He leaned down to cover Bo's mouth with his.

∞

Bo was still shut up in his office when Janine arrived. Sean and Adrian trailed behind her, each carrying a plastic bag in addition to their book bags. Sam peered at Janine through his eyelashes while pretending to read the parapsychology journal in his hands. She looked exhausted and strangely defeated. Sean, in contrast, practically vibrated with eagerness. Adrian looked almost as tired as his mother, in spite of the slight smile on his face.

The knot of dread which had been building in Sam's stomach loosened a little at the sight of both boys unharmed. He wondered why Adrian looked so worn out, but figured it could easily be the stress of catching up at school after a suspension.

"Good afternoon," Danny greeted them. She stood, smiling. "Bo is expecting you. I'll tell him you're here."

Janine's answering smile was tight and, Sam thought, rather sad. "Thank you, Danny."

"Hi, Sam," Sean called, waving.

Sam waved back. "Hi, Sean. Hi, Adrian. Are y'all looking forward to trick-or-treating tonight?"

Sean's face lit up like a floodlight. "Yeah. We're going with you and Dad. I'm gonna be Master Chief."

Shocked, Sam stared at the beaming child. "Huh?"

Sean gave him an incredulous look. "You know, Master Chief. From Halo? The most awesome game *ever*?"

"No, I meant—"

Before Sam could ask why the boys were going to be with him and Bo that night, Bo stepped out of his office. "Janine. Come in."

She shot an uncomfortable glance in Sam's direction. "Actually, I'd like to talk to you and Sam both."

Bo looked as surprised as Sam felt, but he nodded. "Of course. Sam?"

Unsure of what to say, Sam stood and walked over to join Bo in the office doorway. They exchanged a mystified look.

Janine turned to the boys. "You two wait out here, okay? And be good, don't get in anyone's way."

They both nodded. Adrian went straight to one of the chairs beside the front door and plopped into it. Sean sat in the chair beside him, hands clasped in his lap and feet drumming the floor.

Sam smiled to himself as he followed Bo and Janine into Bo's office. Adrian could probably sit there for at least half an hour before he got restless, but Sean would be up and moving within five minutes.

"What did you need to talk to us about?" Bo lowered

himself into his chair. "Sit down, please."

Janine perched on the edge of the offered seat, her back stiff and tense. Sam leaned against the wall instead of standing with Bo behind the desk. Maybe she would be less unpleasant than usual if she didn't feel confronted by their united front.

"I need you to take the boys out tonight," she said, sounding as if the words had been dragged from her. "Lee's sick, and I have to work. I've been granted an interview I've been after for some time, but he'll only let me talk to him tonight."

Bo blinked. "That's it? There's nothing wrong? Nothing's happened?"

She frowned. "No, of course not. What on earth gave you that idea?"

Sam bit his tongue. Berating her for worrying Bo the way she had wouldn't help matters.

"Nothing, I just…" Bo shook his head. "Nothing. Of course we'll take them."

A weird blend of relief and resentment flooded her face. "Good. Thank you. I didn't want them to have to stay home, but there's just no way I can take them and still do this interview. And I *have* to do the interview."

In other words, your career takes precedence over your sons.

Sam kept that to himself. It was unfair and not entirely true, and he knew it. Indulging the thought in his own head felt cathartic, though.

"It's no trouble at all. You know we're happy to take them." Bo stood, smiling. "Anything else we can do?"

"Yes." Janine's gaze cut toward Sam for a second before settling on Bo again. "I don't want any talk about special powers or whatever you think Adrian has. He's having a difficult enough time without the two of you making it worse."

"What do you mean?" Sam blurted, pushing away from the wall. "You just said nothing's happened. What's he been having a hard time with?"

Bo rubbed his fingertips against his temple. "Sam, please."

"Come on, Bo, she just said—"

"He is having a hard time," Janine interrupted, glaring at Sam, "because his family has been broken up and he is trying to deal with his father being...being *gay*, for God's sake, and carrying on with *you*."

Sam bristled, but Bo cut him off before he could say anything. "All right, that's enough." He crossed his arms and aimed a stern look at his ex-wife. "Janine, I think we all realize how hard this whole thing has been for Adrian, but he's adjusting. In any case, I will not apologize for finally being happy, and I most certainly won't apologize for leaving a relationship that was bad for me. One that was just as bad for you, I might add."

Janine dropped her gaze to the floor. Sam stifled a crow of triumph. *Yeah. Suck on that, bitch.*

Before Sam could turn the uncharitable thought into a childish remark, Bo shot him a look suggesting he knew exactly what Sam was thinking and he'd better not say it. Sam dutifully kept his mouth shut.

Sighing, Bo tucked a loose strand of hair behind his ear. "Okay. We all know there are hard feelings here, and we all know why. But we're adults, for God's sake. Surely we can all put our differences aside, at least when Sean and Adrian are around. The three of us fighting can only make things worse for the boys, and they're the only ones who are completely blameless in this situation."

"I hardly think—"

Bo cut off Janine's indignant rejoinder with a single raised finger. "Stop. Just stop. No more fighting. It gets us nowhere."

To Sam's immense surprise, Janine closed her mouth and sat staring at the floor. She looked very much like Sean did whenever Bo reprimanded him.

"That's better." Bo sat on the edge of the desk, cautious gaze darting between Sam and Janine as if he expected one—or both—of them to start a fist fight at any moment. "Janine, do you have the boys' costumes with you?"

She cleared her throat and peered up at Bo. "Yes, the boys have them."

He nodded. "Okay, good. Would you like me to take them straight back to your place after trick-or-treating, or would you rather come pick them up?"

"Well. I, um, I guess it would be best if I come pick them up. I'm not sure how late my interview will go, and I really don't want the two of them running around the house tonight if I'm not there. Lee can barely get out of bed right now, he shouldn't have to wrangle those two when they're on a sugar high. Especially Sean, you know how he gets."

Sam choked back a laugh. "Sorry," he said in response to Janine's narrow-eyed glare. "I was just thinking you're right about Sean, he's a regular human tornado after a few pieces of candy."

A tiny smile tugged up the corners of Janine's mouth. It wasn't much, but it lifted a tremendous weight off Sam's shoulders. He and Janine usually needed only the slightest provocation to snipe at each other. Having a civil exchange, no matter how abbreviated, was a huge step up for them.

The look in Bo's eyes said he'd noticed it too, and applauded the effort on both their parts. Sam smiled at him. *Now if only Bo and Janine can get through this little meeting without screaming at each other, I'll believe in miracles.*

Visibly collecting herself, Janine pushed to her feet. "All right. I need to go. Thank you for doing this, Bo. I know it's last minute, and I...I really appreciate it."

Bo's face lit up. "Believe me, I'm happy to do it." He reached out and took Sam's hand, winding their fingers together. "We both are."

Janine looked away, lips pursing, but said nothing about the small display of affection. "Well. Good." She glanced at their joined hands, looked away again and strode toward the door. "I'll see you later, then. I should be able to pick the boys up by ten thirty at the latest."

"That'll be fine." Bo gave her a wide smile. "See you then. Tell Lee we said hi and we hope he feels better soon."

With a curt nod, Janine pulled the door open and hurried out. Sam didn't follow her. He figured it might be better for all concerned if he stayed out of sight until she left. No point in tempting fate.

Bo squeezed Sam's hand. "Well. *That* was a surprise."

"Yeah. I think this is the closest we've ever come to the three of us being in one room without anyone yelling at anyone else."

Laughing, Bo pulled Sam close and kissed his chin. "I think you're right." He trailed his lips downward and licked at the pulse point in Sam's throat. "This is a big step forward for you and Janine, you know."

"I know." Sam lifted his chin to encourage Bo's kisses. "For you and her too."

"Yes, well, if I'd sniped at her the way I generally want to, she might've changed her mind and taken the boys to Rita's instead, and I didn't want that to happen." Bo drew back to meet Sam's gaze. "I hope we can keep this truce going."

"We will." Cupping Bo's cheek in one hand, Sam captured his mouth in a gentle kiss.

The kiss had just started to heat up when the sound of a throat clearing made them jump apart.

"Sorry to break up the manlove," David said, looking not at all sorry. "But the young'uns want to see their dad."

"Of course." Cheeks flaming, Bo shot Sam an apologetic look before hurrying out to see his sons.

David leaned close to Sam as they followed Bo out of the office. "So. What happened with the dragon lady?"

"Nothing, actually. She was almost pleasant." Sam thought about it. "Okay, well, maybe pleasant is the wrong word. But there was no yelling, and that was a major improvement."

"I'll say." Grinning, David punched him lightly in the arm. "That's awesome, Sam. Maybe she's starting to come around."

"I hope so."

The conversation was cut short when Sean came barreling up and threw himself at Sam so hard Sam staggered backward. Sam hugged the child, who immediately started telling Sam about his successful book report that day.

Straightening up, Sam saw Adrian sitting in the extra chair beside Dean's desk. Bo sat next to him in a chair he'd pulled over from Sam's desk, one arm resting on the boy's shoulders as they talked. Adrian had a shy smile on his face, but there were dark circles under his eyes, and a worried crease marred his forehead.

A renewed sense of disquiet coiled in the pit of Sam's stomach. What had happened in the past few days to make Adrian look like that?

Adrian glanced over and caught Sam's eye. They stared at

each other for a second before Adrian looked away and hunched closer to his father.

I'll talk to him, Sam resolved, taking Sean's hand and leading him over to join the other two. *Tonight. I'll sit him down and try to find out what's been going on.*

It was a good plan. Now all he needed was Adrian's cooperation.

∞

"Come on, Adrian."

"No."

"Please?"

"I told you I don't want to."

"But, Adriaaaaan," Sean whined, grabbing his brother's arm and shaking it. "I don't want to go trick-or-treating by myself. Why won't you come with me?"

"I'll be with you." Bo walked in from his and Sam's bedroom, where he'd been digging a couple of old plastic pumpkin-shaped buckets out of the closet. He handed one to Sean. "Here."

Sean took the pumpkin, still pouting. "It's more fun with Adrian."

Bo ruffled Sean's hair. "He'll be going with us later, when we go around the neighborhood. It's just the trick-or-treating at the mall that he's sitting out."

"Can Sam come with us?"

"Sam is staying with Adrian."

"But, Dad—"

"We talked about this, Sean. Sam needs to stay here with

Adrian so he won't be here by himself. We'll all go around the neighborhood together in a couple of hours, okay?"

"Yeah, okay." With a deep sigh, Sean picked up his Master Chief helmet from the sofa and tucked it under his arm. "All right, Dad. I'm ready."

"Good." Crossing the room to where Sam sat on the couch, Bo bent and gave him a swift kiss, then went to hug Adrian, who was slouched on the loveseat. "We'll be back around seven thirty."

"Have fun," Sam called.

With a brief but meaningful look in Sam's direction, Bo ushered Sean out, and Sam was alone with Adrian.

Sam clasped his hands together. Nervousness made his mouth dry and his palms wet. He and Bo had talked about what to do as soon as Adrian announced, on the trip home, that he didn't want to go trick-or-treating at the mall. They figured Bo could take Sean to the mall and Sam could try to coax Adrian into talking about whatever was bothering him. Bo thought whatever it was had to do with his newly discovered psychokinesis, and Sam agreed.

Being willing to talk to Adrian was one thing. Sam was more than willing. But he'd never been a confidant to a child, and he was terrified of screwing it up.

After a moment's silence, Sam squared his shoulders and met Adrian's guarded gaze. "So. What do you want to do until your dad and brother get back?"

Adrian stared until Sam had to fight the urge to squirm. He wondered if all eleven-year-olds were this intense.

Probably not.

"You said you'd teach me how to control this thing I can do," Adrian said, watching Sam's face. "Can you do that right now?"

Sam's eyebrows shot up. He'd expected to have to draw Adrian out. This was beyond his greatest hopes.

"Uh, sure. Yeah, of course. I'd be happy to." Now was the perfect time to ask Adrian if anything else had happened at home, but he wasn't sure how to ask it. With the silence stretching on, Sam decided to just ask. "Adrian, has anything happened at home? Like the thing here with the light bulb exploding, I mean?"

Adrian's gaze dropped to study the floor. "Kind of."

Sam's stomach rolled. "Can you tell me about it?"

Hunching forward, Adrian clasped his hands together. "There's shadows and sounds and stuff in my room at night. I can't sleep." Adrian lifted his face, fear shining from the big dark eyes. "Sometimes I think I see something there. Like something real. It scares me."

Oh shit. Is he causing portal activity? Or is it just a manifestation of his psychokinesis? There was no way to know for sure without going back to the house and doing a thorough investigation—including psychic scans—while Adrian was there. Broaching that subject with Janine, however, would be pointless at best and an invitation for legal intervention at worst.

Sam kept his expression calm with a huge effort. "Have you told your mom or Lee about those things?"

Adrian shook his head. "Mom wouldn't believe me. She'd just tell me to stop being a baby. Lee would be nice, but he'd tell Mom."

"What about Sean? Has anything happened to him?"

"No. Just me, and just at night when I go to bed." Adrian chewed his lower lip, looking very young and lost. "So, what do I do?"

Sam wanted to ask more questions. He suspected that Adrian was experiencing these things at bedtime because that was the only time he allowed his emotions free reign. On the one hand, it was encouraging to think he'd been practicing the few small hints Sam had given him. On the other hand, the thought of him lying in his bed at night, alone and vulnerable to things he couldn't even imagine, made Sam feel cold inside.

Shaking off the urge to continue his questioning, Sam forced himself to focus on the plans he'd been developing in the past few days for helping Adrian learn to control his abilities. He and Bo could talk about what to do later. Right now, his job was to do his level best to teach Adrian what he could in a limited amount of time.

"Okay," Sam began. "Let's start with some breathing exercises."

Adrian gave him a skeptical look. "Breathing? That's it?"

"No, that's only the beginning. But I'm just now figuring out that I should've started with the simple stuff and moved up from there. I started out with the harder things, and only recently found out how much it helped just to learn how to breathe correctly. It would've made the past few months *much* easier if I'd done that to start with."

"Um. Okay."

Adrian didn't look convinced. Not that Sam blamed him. He wouldn't have believed such at thing at that age either.

"I know it sounds silly, but I promise it'll help. Will you try?"

For a second, Adrian didn't answer. Then he gave a hesitant nod. "Okay."

"Great." Pushing to his feet, Sam gestured toward the

entertainment center. "Why don't you find a CD you like and put it on? Something slow and relaxing."

One of Adrian's eyebrows quirked, making him look even more like Bo than usual. "I'll try to find something." He stood and crossed to the CD cabinet.

While Adrian dug through the music, Sam pulled the coffee table out of the way so that the plush throw rug lay bare in the space between the sofa and love seat. He slipped his sneakers off and sat cross-legged on the rug. Across the room, Adrian slipped a CD into the tray and pushed play. The soft strains of "Dear Prudence" floated through the air.

"Nice music choice," Sam observed as Adrian joined him on the rug.

Adrian shrugged. "I like The Beatles."

"Me too." Sam smiled. "Are you ready?"

Another shrug. "Yeah, I guess."

"Then let's get started."

∞

Adrian took to the breathing exercises like the proverbial duck to water. Watching him, Sam imagined he could actually see the tension easing from the boy's shoulders. When he felt Adrian was sufficiently relaxed to move on, Sam introduced him to some of the basic techniques for focusing the mind and giving direction to the thoughts. Once again, Adrian picked it up easily.

"Why don't we stop for now?" Sam suggested when he sensed Adrian tiring. "Bo and Sean'll be back soon, and you still need to get into your costume."

"Yeah." Uncoiling his legs, Adrian stood and stretched. "Uh, thanks. For showing me that stuff."

"No problem." Sam hauled himself to his feet, wincing at the ache in his knees. "Next time we'll work on some visualization."

Adrian blinked. "Next time?"

"Sure. You can't learn everything you need to know in an hour and a half."

"Oh." Adrian crossed his arms and studied the rug beneath his feet. "So, you're gonna keep on teaching me?"

"Of course." Moving closer, Sam laid a tentative hand on Adrian's arm. "I know I'm not your father, Adrian. But you're Bo's son, so I consider you part of my family. I'll do anything in my power to help you and protect you. Right now, that means teaching you to control this new ability of yours. Okay?"

"Okay." Adrian gave him a small but hopeful smile. "I'm gonna go get on my costume."

"All right." Sam dropped his hand and stepped back. "Yell if you need anything."

Nodding, Adrian dashed off toward the bedroom he and Sean shared. Sam put the coffee table back, then sat on the sofa just as the door opened and Bo and Sean came in.

"Hi," Sam said. "Did y'all have fun?"

"Sean wasn't too happy with the candy haul." Bo shut the door and tucked his keys into his jacket pocket. "But he did win a prize for best costume."

"Yeah, it was awesome!" Tossing his helmet on the floor, Sean bounded over to Sam and held out a slip of paper with the name of a local electronics store on it. "Look, I got a gift certificate."

Sam studied the paper. "Wow, twenty-five dollars. That's

great, Sean."

Sean nodded, grinning ear to ear. "It was cool. The stores at the mall don't have such good candy, though. All I got was Sweet Tarts and Dum Dums and stuff like that. No chocolate at all."

Sam laughed. "Maybe you'll get some chocolate from the people in the neighborhood."

"Your brother likes Sweet Tarts," Bo said, walking over to sit beside Sam. "Why don't you take those to him?"

"'Kay." Sean looked around. "Where is he?"

"In your room." Sam waved a hand toward the hall. "He's getting his costume on."

"Cool, thanks."

Sam chuckled as Sean spun around and raced toward the bedroom. "God, he's an energetic little thing, isn't he?"

"Oh, yes." Taking Sam's hand, Bo wove their fingers together. "So. How'd it go with Adrian?"

"Really well. I taught him those breathing exercises I've been doing lately, then I worked with him on clearing his mind and focusing his thoughts." Sam rubbed his thumb along the back of Bo's hand. "He did great. Much better than I expected. I thought I'd have a hard time getting him to listen to me and work with me, but he was a fantastic student."

Relief washed over Bo's face. "God, I'm glad to hear that. I was worried his usual attitude toward you would get in the way. It's good to know he's able to put all that aside."

"He's a very mature kid. Smart too." Sam leaned closer and lowered his voice. "There's one thing, though. I found out that Adrian's been seeing and hearing things in his room at night."

Bo tensed. "What sorts of things?"

"He just said he'd heard noises, not what kind, but he said

111

he'd seen shadows, and sometimes he thought he'd seen something more solid."

Closing his eyes, Bo sagged against Sam's side. "Christ, Sam. What if—?"

"I know." Sam let go of Bo's hand and slipped his arm around Bo's shoulders instead. "I think we should go back to the house and take another look around, with full psychic sweep, and with Adrian there."

"I think you're right. And if we're going to do that, I think we should do overnight video and audio in Adrian's room. Maybe have you stay in there with him, to see what happens psychically speaking." Bo opened his eyes and turned a solemn, frightened expression to Sam. "How in the hell are we going to convince Janine to let us do that?"

"I've been thinking about that, while Adrian and I were working, and I have an idea."

"What is it?"

"We'll talk to Lee, find a time when Janine won't be home, and do it then. You know she does overnight assignments fairly regularly, so it shouldn't be too hard."

Bo stared at him. "Oh my God, that is so devious."

"Yeah, I know." Sam glanced toward the hallway, where he could hear the boys talking. "So, what do you think?"

"We'll have to be very, very careful to keep Janine from finding out."

"Definitely."

"As a matter of fact, we probably shouldn't tell Sean either. He'll be excited about it, and when he's excited about something he tells everyone in hearing range."

"Hm, good point." Sam frowned. "Is it too risky?"

"It's definitely risky." Bo sucked his bottom lip between his

112

teeth and let it go with a pop. "But I think we should do it. We need more information about what's happening in that house, and the only way to get it is to go there."

Sam gazed at the half-open door to Sean and Adrian's bedroom. "I guess we'll have to talk to Adrian."

"Yes." Bo let out a sigh. "I wish I knew what to tell him. He's already frightened, having him terrified out of his mind by the thought of calling up those...those *things*, would be counterproductive at best. But he'll have to know at least something of what we're doing if he's going to be involved."

"Mm." Sam was silent for a moment, thinking. "What if we tell him we want to investigate the house one more time to see what exactly happens at night when he's seeing things, so we'll know better how to help him? It's true, after all."

Before Bo could answer, Sean and Adrian exited the bedroom, cutting off any further planning. Adrian wore a long black cloak and plastic vampire teeth, and he'd slicked his hair back with gel.

"I'll talk to Adrian when we get back, and I'll call Lee tomorrow," Bo murmured before pulling away from Sam's side and rising to his feet. "All right, boys, are we ready?"

"Yeah, let's go!" Sean dashed over to pick up his helmet and stood bouncing on his toes in front of the door. "Come on, before all the good candy gets gone."

Laughing, Bo held a hand down to help Sam up. "We wouldn't want to miss out on the good candy."

Sam snagged his jacket and shrugged it on. He took Bo's hand as they left the apartment. Bo gave his fingers a grateful squeeze.

Chapter Nine

Bo called Lee at work the next day to explain what he and Sam wanted to do, and why. Though wary of Janine's reaction if she should find out, Lee agreed to let them know the next time she went out of town on assignment.

Sam knew waiting would be difficult. He steeled himself for days—weeks, maybe—of dealing with a tense and worried lover. It surprised both of them when Lee called back a mere two days later, on Thursday afternoon.

"Janine's going to Montgomery tomorrow for an assignment at the state capital building," Bo explained after he hung up the phone.

Sam's pulse picked up. "And Sean?"

"Spending the night with a friend of his." Skirting his desk, Bo walked over to stand beside Sam. "We won't get a better chance than this."

"You're right." Taking Bo's hand, Sam laced their fingers together. "We have a preliminary visit for the downtown library investigation tomorrow, but we should be done before five."

"Good. I'll talk to Andre and we'll work out the details." Bo gazed up at Sam with solemn eyes. "I'm scared, Sam."

"Of what?" Sam asked, though he thought he knew.

"Of what we might find." Bo moved closer, his free hand

creeping around to rest on the small of Sam's back. "What do we do if we find out there's a real danger of a portal opening? How do we get the kids out of there? If we just take Adrian and run, she'll send the police after us and they'll take him straight back there."

The fear in Bo's voice tore at Sam's heart. Releasing Bo's hand, Sam wound both arms around Bo's waist and pulled him close. "We'll think of something. We won't let anything happen to either of those kids. I promise."

Bo couldn't possibly think Sam had the power to keep that promise if they came face to face with another portal, but he clung to Sam as if he believed it with all his heart.

∞

At eight o'clock on Friday night, the BCPI team arrived at Lee and Janine's house. Squeezing six people and all their investigative equipment into Sam's pickup and Dean's Civic wasn't easy, but everyone agreed that more than two vehicles would be even more conspicuous than a company SUV.

Lee came out onto the back porch just as Sam and Dean parked their vehicles in the narrow space to one side of the backyard. "Hi," he greeted them as they grabbed the equipment bags and crossed to the porch. "Come on in."

They all trooped through the back door into the kitchen. Shifting his camera bag to his left hand, Bo stuck out his right hand to shake Lee's. "Thank you so much for helping us do this, Lee. We really appreciate it."

"I'm happy to do it. I'm not sure what's going on with Adrian, but I'd like to make sure he and Sean are safe here." Lee leaned against the wall. "Do you need me for anything?

Because to tell you the truth I'm still not feeling very well."

"You don't need to do a thing," Bo assured him. "Why don't you go lie down?"

"I think I will." Pushing away from the wall, Lee shuffled toward the archway leading into the dining room, the BCPI group trailing behind him. "Let me know if you have any questions or anything. I'll just be watching TV upstairs. That's okay, right? It won't interfere with anything?"

Andre shrugged. "Normally I'd ask you not to, but in this case we want pretty much a normal nighttime environment. So just go about your usual routine."

"Okay." Lee shot a thoughtful look over his shoulder. "Normally we'd all be in the family room at this point, should I go in there instead?"

Bo shook his head. "I don't think that's necessary. Just you being here and going about your business will be enough."

"We're going to do a quick sweep with cameras and EMF, including the family room," Sam added. "We want to see if the EMF in there is within a safe range now that the electrician's been out to fix it."

"It better be, after all the money we spent." Lee stopped in the foyer and gestured up the steps. "All right, I'm going upstairs. Adrian's in the family room, reading. He's kind of nervous about this."

Cecile made a sympathetic noise. "Poor thing, I know this must be scary for him."

"I'm sure. That's why at least one of us will be with him at all times." Bo set his bag on the floor. "Come on, Sam. We'll go talk to him and make sure he's okay with everything."

Dropping his bag of extension cords and batteries, Sam followed Bo into the family room. Adrian lay curled on the sofa, reading *Mrs. Frisbee and the Rats of NIMH*. Sam smiled. He'd loved that book himself when he was Adrian's age.

The boy set his book aside and sat up when his father and Sam entered. "Hi."

"Hi, son." Bo settled beside Adrian and gave him a quick hug. "How have things been the last couple of days?"

"Not so bad." Adrian shot Sam a shy half-smile. "I think the stuff Sam showed me helped."

Pleased, Sam grinned back. "I'm glad, Adrian."

Bo gave Sam a grateful look before turning back to his son. "Okay, I talked to you before about why we wanted to do this, and what we hoped to accomplish. Do you have any questions? Anything you're worried about?"

Adrian chewed on his lower lip for a moment. "Is someone going to stay with me in my room?"

"Absolutely. Only Sam and I are staying overnight, and since Sam has the same abilities we believe you do we thought it would be best for him to camp out in your room."

"Okay." Adrian glanced from his father to Sam and back again. "What about you? Where are you staying?"

"I thought I could stay right here in the family room, on the sofa. I can set up the laptop in here and monitor the cameras remotely." Bo brushed Adrian's bangs out of his eyes. "Is that plan all right with you? We both want you to be comfortable with what we're doing, so if you have different ideas please let us know."

Adrian stared at his lap. "Can you both stay with me? I mean, I know Sam has to stay because he knows about all this weird stuff that happens to me, but I want you with me too. Is that okay?"

The concern on Bo's face melted into an expression of such

tenderness it nearly brought Sam to tears. He felt a wave of fierce gratitude toward Adrian for making Bo so happy.

"Of course that's okay," Bo answered, his voice shaking just a little. "We can put the laptop in the hallway outside your room and take turns monitoring it. You won't have to be alone at all."

Adrian's relief was clear in his eyes. He nodded. "So what happens now? Can I help with investigating?"

Bo darted a questioning look in Sam's direction. Sam shrugged. Personally, he thought it might be good for the boy to be involved in the work, but the final decision was Bo's.

"I don't see why not." Bo pushed to his feet. "Come on, we'll show you the equipment we're going to use and how to work it, and you can help Sam and me take video and EMF readings in your room."

Adrian's face lit up. "Cool." He jumped up from the sofa to follow his dad into the hall. "I want to do the EMF, can I?"

Laughing, Bo rested an arm across Adrian's shoulders. "Sure."

Sam trailed behind them, smiling. Adrian hung on his father's every word, his face the picture of rapt attention as Bo explained how to perform an EMF sweep. It was good to see the boy so excited about something. After all the upheaval in his life lately, he deserved to feel in control of something for a change.

They found the rest of the group clustered around the dining room table, sorting and distributing equipment. David glanced up and grinned as they walked in. "Hey, guys. Have we gained a new investigator?"

"Yes." Bo patted Adrian's back. "Adrian is going to help Sam and me do the initial sweep of his room and decide where to set up the recording equipment there."

"Very cool." Jogging around the table to where Bo and Adrian stood, David held out his hand. "Good to have you on board, Adrian."

The boy took David's hand and shook. "Thanks."

Sam grinned at Adrian's red cheeks and somewhat embarrassed smile. "We need a video camera and EMF detector for the sweep, are they all set?"

"Just about." Dean switched on one of the EMF detectors and studied the display. Nodding, he handed it across the table to Sam. "Here. Fully charged and ready to go."

"And here's a camera." Cecile held out one of the new video cameras to Bo. "You have a full charge on this as well."

"Thank you." Bo turned to Andre, who was fiddling with one of the other cameras. "Andre and Cecile, could I speak with the two of you in private for a minute?"

Andre's eyebrows went up. He exchanged a questioning glance with Cecile, who shook her head. "Sure," Andre answered. He motioned Bo toward the kitchen. "What's up?"

The three of them moved out of hearing range, but Sam had a feeling he knew what Bo wanted. Andre and Cecile were both powerful psychics. Bo needed them to keep their psychic senses wide open, but he didn't want to tell them that—or why he wanted it—in front of Adrian. It would only frighten the boy to know how worried his father was about his safety.

"What're they talking about?"

Jarred from his thoughts, Sam looked down into Adrian's upturned face. "I don't know," he said, truthfully enough. "Probably just giving them instructions about something or other. He does that all the time."

Adrian looked skeptical. "So he's not, like, telling them to be nice to the kid or anything?"

The cynicism in the boy's voice surprised Sam. "No, I don't think he's saying anything like that at all." He wanted to ask why Adrian would think that, but decided against it. In the past few days, Adrian had stopped treating him like the enemy. Sam liked that change, and didn't want to do anything to jeopardize it.

Adrian pursed his lips, but didn't answer.

Bo, Andre and Cecile returned a moment later. Cecile and Andre went to the dining table, while Bo walked over to Sam and Adrian. "Okay, are y'all ready to get started?"

Sam turned a questioning look to Adrian, who nodded eagerly. "Ready, Dad."

Smiling, Bo gave Adrian's shoulder a squeeze. "Then let's head upstairs."

Adrian led the way up the steps. Bo and Sam trailed behind him, carrying the camera and EMF detector.

Halfway up, Bo curled his hand around Sam's. "Tell me everything's going to be okay."

"Everything's going to be okay."

"Thanks."

Sam squeezed Bo's fingers, and Bo shot him a halfhearted smile. With any luck, Sam's little white lie would turn out to be the truth after all.

∞

Within fifteen minutes, Adrian had learned how to read the EMF detector and gotten the hang of using it. While Bo took baseline video, Adrian scanned the room in the slow, methodical manner Bo had taught him, his face screwed up in concentration.

Sam watched the two of them with half an eye while he sent psychic feelers through the room. It was nice to see father and son working together, especially after the tension between them during the past few months. He hoped it would continue.

As he psychically probed the bedroom, his mind caught on something and stumbled. Frowning, he felt back along his mental path. And there it was. A fracture in the substance of reality. Thin as a hair, nearly unrecognizable amongst the pulsing energy of a house full of people. In fact, Sam figured he'd have missed it altogether if it hadn't felt so familiar.

He rubbed a hand over his eyes. *Shit.*

"Sam?"

Shaking himself, Sam met Bo's gaze. "Yeah?"

"We've done an initial sweep." Bo sat in the chair at Adrian's desk, the camera in his lap. "What did you feel?"

Yeah, Sam, what did you feel? He wasn't sure how to answer that question, especially with Adrian right there. They'd agreed not to mention the portals, or the creatures which populated the unknown dimension beyond them. But what Sam had just felt meant they might have to re-think things.

"I felt…" Sam glanced at Adrian, who'd just set the EMF detector on his bedside table and run across the hall to the bathroom. "I felt something."

Bo's smile faded. "Something? Like what?"

Sam leaned forward, dropping his voice to a near whisper. "There's an anomaly in the energy here. It might be nothing," he added when Bo went alarmingly pale. "But it did feel kind of familiar. From *other places*, if you know what I mean."

"Yeah. I know. Christ." Bo blew out a long breath. "Did you feel it last time we were here?"

"No."

"Should we get Cecile or Andre to come up?"

Sam thought about it. "If we can get Cecile to come upstairs, she could feel it out from one of the other rooms without having to come into this one. I still don't think we should alarm Adrian if we don't have to."

"Okay. When we get ready to set up cameras, I'll go downstairs and talk to Cecile."

Glancing toward the door, Sam leaned closer to Bo. "What about you? Have you felt anything like...like you did at Fort Medina?"

It still made Sam's stomach churn to think about those frightening days back in May—the changes in Bo when those things invaded his mind, the way they'd manipulated him into serving as a temporary portal focus. Bo had almost died for the second time in only a few months, and Sam didn't think he'd ever truly get over it.

The worst part was, the chemical which had made it possible for the creatures to track Bo was still in his system. As far as they knew, only the anticonvulsant Bo took every night kept it from reactivating. Sam still woke in the night sometimes, terrified that the otherdimensional beings would find Bo again, and take him.

"I didn't feel anything. Not even a tiny twinge." Bo touched Sam's cheek. "I'm okay, Sam. I promise."

Sam turned his head to kiss Bo's palm. He wanted to pull Bo into his arms and just hold him, but was stopped by Adrian entering the room. He wandered over and plopped onto his bed. "What're y'all talking about?"

Bo gave him an obviously forced smile. "Nothing, son. Just work stuff. What did you find on your EMF sweep?"

"It was four, mostly. Sometimes it was a little lower, and right by my closet it was four point seven, but mostly it was right at four." Adrian frowned at his father. "Are you okay, Dad? You look a little sick."

"I'm fine." Patting Adrian's shoulder, Bo stood and set his camera on the desk. "So, Adrian. Where do you think we should put the cameras to record tonight?"

Adrian's eyes saucered. "I get to pick?"

"Well, Sam and I will help position the cameras to get the best angle, but yes, I'd like you to tell us what parts of the room we need to record. You're the most familiar with this room, and you're the only one who knows exactly what all you've seen and where, so who better to decide the best place to put them?"

Adrian's expression barely changed, but the spark in his eyes spoke volumes. Jumping up, he crossed the room to stand in the doorway. "I think you ought to record my bed," he said after a moment's thought. "It'll be kind of weird to have a camera on me while I'm sleeping, but I always hear stuff around my bed, really close to me, and sometimes the shadows are right there by the bed too."

Bo nodded. "Okay. Anyplace else?"

"The closet." Adrian shuffled closer to his father. "That's where I saw the...the thing."

"You mean the thing you said looked solid rather than shadowy?" Sam asked, making sure to keep the shiver of fear inside him out of his voice.

Adrian nodded. "Yeah."

"All right. We'll record the closet too." Bo looked over at Sam. "Would you mind fetching the equipment we'll need? We can set up, then get settled for the night."

"Sure." Sam rose and headed for the door. "You want me

to, um, ask Cecile and Dean to investigate the other upstairs rooms while I'm down there?"

"That would be good, thanks."

Sam looked back. His gaze locked with Bo's. For a moment they stood there staring into each other's eyes, a wealth of questions and apprehension passing unspoken between them. Then Bo blinked and turned away. Sam hurried to the stairs before he could give in to the urge to kiss away the distress in Bo's eyes.

In the dining room, he found David and Andre pacing the periphery of the room with a camera and EMF detector. They both looked up when he entered.

"Hey, Sam," David greeted. "What's up?"

"I'm looking for Cecile." Sam glanced behind him, to where Dean's laughter floated from the family room. "Is she back there with Dean?"

Andre nodded. "They're checking out the area that had such a high EMF before. Should be done in a minute."

David looked up from the video camera he held. "Anything we can do, or you need Cecile in particular?"

"I kind of need Cecile. She has the most precise control over her psychic abilities."

Lowering his EMF detector, Andre gave Sam a curious look. "Did you find something up there?"

"Maybe. I'm not sure."

Understanding dawned in Andre's eyes. "Oh, I see. If it's *that*, she'd be the best one to double check you."

"Yeah." Sam wheeled around to cross the foyer. "See y'all later."

"Good luck," David called.

Waving over his shoulder, Sam headed down the hallway to

the back of the house. He found Dean and Cecile huddled together in front of the entertainment center. "Hi, guys."

Dean lifted his head and gave Sam his usual dazzling smile. "Hey, Sam."

"The EMF's still a bit on the high side," Cecile said, studying the display in her hand. "But it's much better. Down to seven now."

"I'd say that's better." Sam moved closer. "Could y'all come do the upstairs before you finish up down here?"

The two looked at each other. Dean shrugged. "Sure. How come?"

"I felt something strange a few minutes ago, in Adrian's room, and it felt...pretty familiar, if you know what I mean." He glanced at Cecile. "I need you to check it for me, Cecile. You're the only psychic here with enough control to examine the energy in Adrian's room without actually going in there."

"You don't want to scare Adrian," Cecile guessed.

"Right. He's a really smart kid, though. If you just come upstairs and stand outside his room, he'll know something's up."

"But if we go up there together with our equipment and start doing our thing, it'll just be part of the investigation and he won't suspect anything." Dean nodded. "Makes sense to me."

Cecile's brows drew together. "So, you suspect there might be a danger of portals here?"

"I hate to say it, but yes, I do." Sam rubbed the back of his neck. "I could be wrong, though. Which is why I'd like your opinion."

"All right." Cecile switched off the EMF detector. "Should we go up now?"

"Yeah. I just need to grab a couple of cameras and the

cables from the dining room first."

Dean and Cecile followed Sam into the dining room. David raised his eyebrows as Sam fished the necessary cords and a roll of duct tape out of the bag on the floor. "Weren't you just here?"

"Yes, but I forgot to get the stuff I needed when I was in here before." Slinging the cords around his neck and slipping the tape roll over one wrist, Sam straightened up and grabbed two of the stationary cameras from the table. "I'll come back for the laptop in a minute."

"I'll bring it up," Dean offered. "Did Bo decide to set it up upstairs instead of the family room?"

"Yeah. Adrian wanted him to stay in his room with him, so Bo decided we could put the laptop in the hallway and take turns watching it."

"Oh. Cool." Lifting the laptop bag from the floor, Dean hung the strap over one shoulder. "You got all the cords you need?"

"Yeah. Let's go."

Sam trudged up the stairs with Cecile and Dean trailing behind him. On the upstairs landing, Dean set the laptop bag against the wall. "Y'all holler if you need help setting up, okay?"

Sam nodded. "Sure thing. Thanks, guys."

"No problem." Cecile took his hand and gave it a quick squeeze before following Dean into Sean's room.

Plastering a bland smile onto his face, Sam walked into Adrian's room. He set the cameras, cords and duct tape on the desk. "Okay, I brought the cameras, power cords and cables to connect to the laptop. The laptop's out in the hall. Oh, and Cecile and Dean came up with me. They're in Sean's room."

Bo nodded. "Great, Sam, thank you. Let's get these cameras set up. Then I think we should try a test."

"What kind of test?" Adrian asked from his perch in the middle of his bed.

Bo went to sit beside his son. "I think we should try to see what happens when you're alone in your room, and you get upset and frustrated about things. That's when you see the shadows and hear the noises, isn't it?"

Adrian didn't answer that question, but the near panic in his eyes was answer enough. "You said I wouldn't be alone. You said you'd stay with me."

"I will. Sam and I will be right here the whole time." Bo glanced over at Sam. "We won't leave you by yourself. But the whole point of tonight's investigation is to see if we can find out what exactly is going on in here at night, and in order to do that we need to recreate the conditions as precisely as we can in a controlled way. Do you understand?"

Sam thought there was no way he himself would've understood that at eleven, but Adrian nodded as if it were all perfectly clear. "Uh-huh. So what do we do?"

"Let's see." Bo rubbed his chin, brow furrowed in thought. "We should set up everything first. After that, you should get in bed and get comfortable, just as if you were getting ready to go to sleep any other night. Then just shut your eyes and let your mind wander. Pretend Sam and I aren't here, that the cameras aren't here, think about all the hard things in your life and just...let yourself get angry."

Adrian's throat worked. "What if something happens?"

The tremor in the boy's voice brought out protective instincts Sam hadn't even known he had. "Your dad and I will be right here. We won't let anything hurt you."

Bo's eyes widened, and Sam realized—too late—that he'd basically just told Adrian this might be dangerous. Thankfully, Adrian seemed to latch onto the promise of protection rather than the idea that he might *need* protecting.

Of course, Adrian might have known all along that he was in danger. Such a perceptive child wouldn't question the instinctive feeling of threat.

"Sam's right. Nothing's going to happen to you." Bo pushed to his feet. "Let's get started setting up. Adrian, would you mind running downstairs and bringing up a folding chair or something? We can put the laptop on that little table in the hall, but we'll need a place to sit while we're watching it."

"All right." With a narrow-eyed glance at his father, Adrian sauntered out of the room.

The second he was gone, Bo went straight to Sam and clutched him in a tight embrace. Sam wrapped both arms around Bo, one hand stroking up and down his back. Neither spoke. They didn't need to. Both knew what they might have to face.

The sound of footsteps thumping up the stairs announced Adrian's imminent arrival. Bo drew out of Sam's arms, took one of the cameras and started hooking up cables.

Meeting Adrian's nervous gaze with a smile, Sam took the other camera and crossed to the shelf on the other side of Adrian's room, beside his closet. "What do you think, Adrian? Would this shelf be a good spot to film your bed?"

The boy watched with a thoughtful expression as Sam nudged aside a couple of Star Wars action figures and set the camera on the shelf. "Probably. How do you tell if it's right?"

"We'll connect the cameras to the laptop," Bo answered. "Then we'll be able to see what they're recording on the laptop display."

"Oh. Okay." Adrian leaned the folding chair he carried against the wall. "You want me to help connect the cords and stuff? I know how."

Bo's eyebrows went up. "Where'd you learn that?"

"In school. We have computer classes, and my teacher showed us how to hook up different things." Adrian shrugged. "We haven't done cameras, but I bet I could figure it out."

"This one's ready to connect," Sam said, securing the cord to the camera. "Why don't you and Adrian go on and boot up the laptop while I double check the cameras, then y'all can connect both of them?"

"That sounds fine." Bo squeezed Adrian's shoulder. "Come on, son. Bring that chair out in the hall, please."

Adrian hefted the chair and followed his father into the hallway. Their voices floated back to Sam as he inspected the cameras to make sure both cables were properly plugged in. He looked up when he heard Cecile and Dean greeting Bo and Adrian.

"Hey," he said as Cecile entered the room. Dean remained in the hall, talking. "Anything interesting next door?" He kept his voice as casual as he could make it, but a thread of tension still ran through it. Maybe Adrian would be too busy to notice.

"Nothing, really. EMF's about the same level as the rest of the house." With a glance over her shoulder, Cecile sidled close to Sam and lowered her voice to a whisper. "I felt it, Sam. It's hard to pick out, but it's there."

"Did it feel like a potential portal to you?"

She nodded, dark eyes wide and solemn. "It's hard to say if it's ever been active, or is ever likely to become active, but the potential is there, in my opinion."

"Shit."

"Absolutely."

Sam glanced over Cecile's shoulder at the doorway, where Dean was making Adrian laugh with a particularly juvenile joke. "Do you think he's in danger?"

"Honestly? I have no idea." Frowning, Cecile bit her lip. "My gut says he's in no immediate danger, but I could be wrong. I could also be wrong about there being any danger at all. You know how inexact this whole psychic thing is."

"You got that right." Sam rubbed his eyes, feeling dead tired all of a sudden. "I know the rest of you had planned to leave once the initial sweep was done, but do you think you could stay for a little longer? Once the cameras and laptop are set up, Bo wants to try seeing what happens when Adrian gets angry. We need to do that, but I'll feel a lot better if everyone's here in the house during that test. You and Andre will know if something's going wrong, and y'all can help us get Lee and Adrian out safe."

"I'll talk to Andre, but I'm sure that won't be a problem." Rising on tiptoe, Cecile kissed Sam's cheek, then pulled him into a quick hug. "Would you like me to let Bo know what I found, or would you rather do it?"

"I'll do it." Sam gave her a halfhearted smile as she drew away. "Thanks, Cecile."

"No problem." She patted his arm. "We'll be downstairs. One of you come down and let us know once you've concluded your testing, okay?"

"Sure."

He lowered himself onto the edge of Adrian's bed as Cecile left the room. His heart thudded hard and fast against his sternum. Knowing what he'd felt was real terrified him. What the hell would they do if this "test" of Bo's let loose something they still weren't one hundred percent sure how to fight?

Bo's head popped around the doorframe. "Sam, could you move the desk camera a little to the right?"

"Yeah." Hopping to his feet, Sam walked to the desk and

repositioned the camera. "How's that?"

"A little more," Bo called from the hall, where he'd gone back to the laptop.

Sam moved the camera a bit more, stopping when Bo gave the word. He grabbed the roll of duct tape and secured the cord in place on the desk. "Is the other camera okay?"

"Yes, it's perfect where it is." Bo came through the doorway with Adrian at his side. "Adrian, go ahead and get changed and get your teeth brushed. Then we'll get started."

"Okay." Darting a quick look at Sam, Adrian opened his top dresser drawer, dug out a pair of Darth Maul pajamas and left the room.

Bo turned to Sam with eyes full of curiosity and dread. "What did Cecile say?"

"She felt the same thing as I did."

"And she agrees about what it might be?"

Sam nodded. Bo swore. "Maybe we should call off the test phase."

"We'll do whatever you think is best. But Cecile said she'd talk to Andre and have the whole group stay until we're ready to settle in for the night. That way, if anything *did* happen, they'd be here, and could help protect Adrian and Lee."

Bo pulled his braid over his shoulder. He wound the end around his hand, unwound it, wound it up again. "Okay. We'll go ahead and do the test as planned. If anything is going to happen, I'd much rather it happened while we're here and more or less prepared for it."

"Exactly." Sam untangled Bo's hand from his braid and kissed the inside of his wrist. "I think maybe having us here will temper Adrian's emotions enough to keep anything much from happening anyway."

"That's true." Bo glanced toward the hallway, then tilted his head up and captured Sam's mouth in a swift kiss which contained more need for comfort than anything else. When they pulled apart, Bo pinned Sam with a pleading stare. "Are you ready for this?"

The questions Bo hadn't asked came through loud and clear. *Are you ready for what might happen tonight? Are you ready to face a monster if need be, to save my son's life?*

Mustering as much confidence as he could, Sam nodded. "Yes."

Chapter Ten

While Bo sat on the edge of Adrian's bed and talked to him in an attempt to relax him, Sam crossed the hall to let Lee know about their plans. He and Bo both figured Lee should be told what they wanted to do and why, and be given veto power should he choose it.

Lee looked paler than ever by the time Sam finished explaining everything, but readily agreed that Bo's plan was for the best. To Sam's relief, Lee decided to go downstairs with the rest of the crew. Adrian was as well protected as humanly possible, and in spite of his strained relationship with Lee, the child would never get over it if Lee was harmed. He would blame himself, and the guilt would swallow him whole.

Back in Adrian's room, Sam found Bo seated at the desk, out of the camera's line of sight. The overhead light was off, and Bo had switched on a nightlight. He looked up as Sam entered. Rising, he went to stand beside the bed, where Adrian lay staring at the ceiling. "Sam's going to sit with you for a little bit, son. I'll be right outside, watching the camera displays on the laptop."

Adrian's eyes cut toward his father. "So we're starting now?"

"Yes." Leaning down, Bo kissed his son's forehead. "Just relax, and let your thoughts flow like they usually do."

Nodding, Adrian shut his eyes. Bo straightened up and met Sam at the door. His hand closed around Sam's wrist, clutching hard enough to hurt. He didn't say anything, but the fear in his eyes spoke for itself.

Sam dipped his head to plant a light kiss on Bo's mouth. "It'll be okay," he whispered. "I love you."

Bo's lips curved into the slightest of smiles. Letting go of Sam's wrist, he strode out into the hall, leaving Sam alone with Adrian and the possibilities of what he could do.

After a few minutes of fidgeting, Adrian sat up with a sigh, rubbing his eyes. "This sucks. I can't get comfortable."

"That's okay. You don't really need to be comfortable for this part."

"Dad said I had to relax."

"I know. But only enough to kind of let your thoughts and emotions go. We don't want you going to sleep just yet."

The boy leveled a mulish glare at Sam. "I wasn't going to."

"I'm sure you weren't." Leaning forward, Sam rested his elbows on his knees. "Listen, why don't you try some of those breathing exercises I showed you? That should relax you enough to let you stop trying so hard and just let it happen. Okay?"

Adrian looked skeptical, but didn't argue. Plopping backward onto his pillow, he shut his eyes and began the slow, rhythmic breathing Sam had taught him. Within a couple of minutes, the furrows smoothed from Adrian's brow. Not long after that, his fingers began to pick at the quilted comforter.

With a quick glance toward the desk to make sure he wasn't blocking the camera, Sam slid to the edge of his chair, his gaze fixed on Adrian. The child's nose wrinkled. One small fist bunched the material of his pajamas. He seemed to be almost in a trance. *An angry trance,* Sam amended, watching the boy's top lip curl in an unconscious sneer. He wondered what Adrian was thinking about.

Something flickered at the edge of Sam's vision. He whipped his head around. Amid the shadows of the open closet, a deeper darkness swirled and vanished before Sam could determine its shape.

Sam stared into the clutter of books, toys and clothes. Nothing moved. Cautiously, he let his mind ease open. The fracture he'd noticed before remained unchanged, though it was easier for him to pick it out this time. He took a slow, deep breath, then another, allowing his senses to expand. Tendrils of his thought sifted through the normal energy of the house, searching for whatever might lie beneath.

A cold alien presence brushed Sam's aura like icy fingers. Startled, he grasped at it with his mind. It slipped away from him and was gone as swiftly as it had appeared.

Heart hammering, Sam leaned back in his chair. He felt dirty, as if the thing which had just slithered through his consciousness had left an oily residue behind. He had no idea what to do now. Should he tell Bo what he'd felt? Should they cut their test short? Or was he letting his past experiences with the portals skew his objectivity?

As if in answer to his question, darkness coalesced into a near-solid mass in the depths of Adrian's closet. Something shifted and clattered to the floor.

Adrian shot to a sitting position, breathing hard. "What was that?" The boy's voice shook.

"I don't know." Jumping up, Sam flipped the switch to turn on the overhead light. Was it his imagination, or did the churning blackness linger for a moment before fading in the brightness? "Did you see anything?"

"Yeah. It was—"

The bedroom door flew open, cutting Adrian off. "What happened?" Bo demanded, his gaze darting between Sam and Adrian.

Sam gave Bo a surreptitious once-over. Bo's voice was calm, but Sam saw the pure terror lurking behind his carefully controlled expression. "Something in Adrian's closet fell."

"There was something in there," Adrian chimed in. "I saw it."

Sam answered the question in Bo's eyes with a tiny shake of his head. *Later,* he mouthed. He didn't want to discuss what he'd felt in front of Adrian. Not without talking to Bo alone first.

With a swift but meaningful look at Sam to indicate he understood, Bo crossed the room to perch on the edge of his son's mattress. "What did you see, Adrian?"

"It was the thing. The solid one." He screwed his mouth sideways in thought. "Or, well, almost. It wasn't quite solid yet. But it was gonna be in a second."

Sam and Bo glanced at each other. "So this was the same thing you've seen before?" Bo asked, watching Adrian's face.

"Uh-huh." Adrian drew both legs up, wrapped his arms around them and rested his chin on his knees. He stared at his father with solemn eyes. "What was it, Dad? Can we make it go away?"

Bo gave him a strained smile. "Let's look at the videos before we start making plans, okay?"

"But, Dad, what if it's...?" Adrian scooted closer to Bo. "What if it's a monster, Dad? Like the one that bit you?" The boy's voice quavered just a little.

Bo glanced up at Sam, his indecision clear in his face. His eyes pleaded with Sam to give him some guidance. To tell him whether he should be completely honest with Adrian, or gloss over the potential danger in order to allay his fears. Sam shook his head. He wished he had an answer for Bo, but he didn't. Both courses of action held their own particular hazards.

Not knowing what else to do, Sam walked over to sit on Bo's other side. He rested his hand on the small of Bo's back, fingers rubbing soothing circles just above the waistband of Bo's jeans. "Whatever you think, Bo," he murmured.

Sighing, Bo wound an arm around Adrian's shoulders and hugged him close. "Adrian, I know you're anxious to stop seeing and hearing things. But we need to have some sort of proof that something was actually there before we can decide what to do."

Adrian squirmed loose of Bo's embrace. "I saw it. It was there, and it was *real.*"

"Nobody's doubting that you saw something. All I'm saying is that we need to try and find out exactly what it is you saw." Bo reached out to brush a tentative hand across his son's arm. "Sometimes the darkness can play tricks on your eyes. Especially when you're already scared."

Sam winced. He knew Bo didn't want to frighten Adrian, but making him angry was hardly better.

Adrian jumped to his feet, his expression stormy. "I *saw* it! I see it *all the time!* It's not my imagination!"

Bo stood, one hand held out in a placating gesture. "I'm not saying—"

"Yes you are." Adrian backed up, his features contorted in fury. "I thought you believed me, but you don't. *Nobody* does."

Whirling around, Adrian snatched a miniature spaceship off the bedside table and hurled it against the wall. It shattered, sending shards of gray and white plastic skittering across the floor.

Hard on the heels of Adrian's outburst came a low, rusty noise that raised all the hairs along Sam's arms. All other sound and movement stopped cold as Sam, Adrian and Bo turned to stare into the closet, from which the noise had come. The walls seemed to bend inward toward a faint, misty whorl barely visible against the tangle of jackets and shirts.

Sam stared. He felt like all the air had been sucked from his lungs. A horribly familiar pressure throbbed inside his skull. The overhead light flickered and dimmed. Through the static in his mind, Sam heard the rough subterranean snarl once more. It was louder than before.

Fuck. Oh, fuck.

With no time to consider his options—if there even *were* any—Sam focused on the thing trying to force its way between dimensions and pushed. The presence resisted him. Squeezing his eyes shut, Sam shoved with all his strength. For a breathless moment, nothing happened. Then the electricity in the air dissipated, the creeping shadows giving way to the renewed glow of the light.

Sam leaned forward, elbows on knees and head hanging down, panting like he'd just run a marathon. He heard Bo's voice, speaking to Adrian in soothing tones. Adrian himself was silent. Raising his head with an effort, Sam studied the boy. He stood stiff and unmoving, hands loose at his sides, ignoring his father's arms clutching him. His gaze caught and held Sam's. The dark eyes glittered with a palpable terror.

One arm still around Adrian's shoulders, Bo steered the child back to the bed. They both sat, with Adrian sandwiched between Bo and Sam.

Bo reached over to touch Sam's cheek. "Sam? Are you all right?"

Sam managed a wan smile. "Yeah. Hey, I'm getting better at

this."

"That was a monster coming out," Adrian whispered, staring at the floor. "Don't tell me it wasn't, 'cause I know it was. Sam made it go away."

Bo closed his eyes for a second. When he opened them again, the fear in them tore at Sam's heart. Leaning over, Bo kissed the top of Adrian's head. "We think they're from another dimension. Sometimes they find ways to come through to our world. Not often, but once in a while. Sam's psychokinesis gives him the ability to send them back, and to close the portals they use to get here."

Adrian's head snapped up toward Sam, his expression full of hope. "Did you close this one?"

Looking into the child's pleading face, Sam wanted to lie. But he couldn't, for reasons too numerous to count. "No, Adrian, I didn't."

Adrian's shoulders sagged. "Why not?"

"I don't know. That is," Sam clarified in answer to Adrian's puzzled frown, "I'm still not sure why I can close a portal for good when it's all the way open, but not when it isn't."

"We still don't know very much about the portals," Bo added. "All we know for sure is that psychokinesis like you and Sam have seems to give some people the ability to manipulate them."

Adrian's brow furrowed. "You mean I might be able to do like Sam? I might be able to make the monsters go away too?"

Sam and Bo shared a helpless look. Adrian clearly had the ability to open portals by accident, but Sam had no clue as to the true extent of the boy's talents. Would he be able to learn enough control to keep from opening a portal every time the conditions were right? If not, would he have the power to close them again and survive with his sanity intact, as Sam had? Or would he end up as a vegetable like so many others? Sam had no answer to those questions, and no way of finding one without exposing Adrian and everyone around him to a horrific danger.

He might even end up dead, a tiny voice whispered in the back of Sam's mind. *Just because those things haven't harmed you doesn't mean they won't hurt Adrian.*

"We don't know," Bo answered eventually. "It's possible, but..."

But it's also possible that the monsters will destroy you and everyone you love, Sam mentally filled in when Bo trailed off.

Judging by the renewed alarm in Adrian's eyes, he'd heard what Bo hadn't quite said just as clearly as Sam had. "I want to go stay with you and Sam."

Bo chewed his lower lip. The war in his mind was plain on his face. Would it be better to take Adrian away and risk legal action, or leave him here with the threat of the portals and the creatures on the other side looming over him?

Adrian evidently read his father's hesitation as a decision to leave him. He clutched at Bo's arm. "Please, Dad. I don't want to stay here. I'm scared."

The sight of fearful tears welling in Adrian's eyes seemed to shatter Bo's indecision. He tightened his arm around Adrian, holding the boy close. "Okay. You can go home with us tonight. We can have you back before your mother gets home."

"No, I want to stay with you for good." Adrian curled against Bo's side. His knuckles were white where his small hand fisted in Bo's shirt. "If I stay here, the monsters'll get loose. I know they will."

"Son, I—"

Adrian let out a little whimper and buried his face in Bo's

shoulder. "Please, Dad. Please. Don't make me stay here."

Sam met Bo's pained gaze over the top of Adrian's head. His transparent terror, so unlike his usual stoicism, made Sam want to scoop the boy up and hide him away. At that moment, he felt he'd do almost anything to protect Adrian. How much harder must it be for Bo to listen to his child beg him for something he couldn't give, no matter how much he wanted to?

Winding both arms around Adrian's tense little body, Bo hugged him tight, resting his cheek against Adrian's hair. "I'll talk to your mother, okay?"

Adrian nodded. He sniffed deeply, some of the tightness easing from his back and shoulders. "Can we go now?"

"Okay." Bo pushed Adrian gently back to look him in the eye. "You get your things together while Sam and I take down the equipment."

Adrian jumped up, his relief clear in his face, and fished a duffle bag from beneath his bed. While he went to his dresser and started pulling out clothes, Bo and Sam set to work taking down the cameras.

Sam watched Bo from the corner of his eye as they worked. Bo's shoulders were hunched, his face gray and lined with worry. He looked as heartsick as Sam knew he felt. Sam wanted nothing more than to hold him, caress the tautness from his back and kiss away his anxiety.

When Adrian ran across the hall to get his toothbrush and change back into his clothes, Sam saw his chance. He dropped the cord he'd been holding on the desk, went to Bo and folded him in a tight embrace.

With a soft, distressed sound, Bo leaned into Sam's arms, clinging as if Sam were the only thing keeping him attached to the earth. "Fuck, Sam, I'm so scared."

"I know." Sam turned his head and pressed a soft kiss to

Bo's temple. "I'll keep working with him. Tonight, and tomorrow morning, and as often after that as I can. Maybe we can sneak him over to our place for a couple of hours after school sometimes."

"Maybe so." Bo lifted his head to meet Sam's gaze. "It isn't enough."

"No. But it's all we have." Sam leaned his forehead against Bo's. "I don't guess there's any way you can actually talk Janine into letting him stay with us."

Bo let out a bitter laugh. "No way in hell. I'll try, but it won't work. I just hope Adrian doesn't tell her *why* he wants to live with us now."

"He's a smart boy. He knows telling his mom'll just make things worse."

Bo didn't answer. Molding one hand to Sam's cheek, Bo brought their mouths together in a soft kiss. Sam shut his eyes and let himself relax into it. The warmth of Bo's lips against his soothed his jangled nerves, and he knew Bo felt the same.

The sound of footsteps and soft conversation mounted the stairs. Sam and Bo drew apart just as Andre, David and Lee appeared in the doorway. "So what happened?" David asked, darting a curious look around the room. "Andre and Cecile both felt some serious vibes from up here."

Bo shot a swift glance at Lee, who looked pale and shaky. "Adrian almost opened a portal. By accident, of course. Sam stopped it."

Lee went chalk white. He leaned against the doorframe. "Christ."

Frowning, Andre crossed his arms over his stomach. "I was afraid you were going to say that."

"So you felt it?" Sam asked, securing his arm around Bo's

waist.

"Cecile and I both did, yeah."

David gestured toward the two cameras and their associated cords on the desk. "Are y'all done, then?"

"Yes." Bo's hand crept around Sam's back, fingers digging into his hipbone. "Lee, Sam and I are taking Adrian home with us, for tonight at least."

Lee nodded, his shell-shocked expression not changing a bit. "I think that's a good idea."

"Dad?" Adrian slipped through the crowd in his room to Bo's side. He'd changed into jeans, sneakers and an Auburn Tigers sweatshirt. "I'm ready to go. My bag's in the hall."

Bo smiled down at him. "All right. Give us a little while to get everything put away."

Adrian nodded, but Sam could read his fear in the set of his shoulders. Getting Adrian out of the room right now would be a good idea. Sam didn't want a repeat of what had happened a few minutes ago. Things might not end as well this time.

He was really interested in the investigative process before. Maybe that could distract him while we finish breaking down.

Sam laid a hand on Adrian's shoulder. "Hey, why don't you and I head on downstairs? You can help us put away the other equipment, and while we do that I can show you how we use those things to investigate hauntings."

Adrian's face lit up. "That would be cool."

"All right, let's go." Sam nudged Bo's arm. "Okay with you?"

"Of course." Bo leaned over to brush a swift kiss across Sam's mouth. "Thank you, Sam."

Adrian wrinkled his nose. "Eww, kissing."

Across the room, David laughed. "Tell me about it."

Shaking his head, Sam gave Bo's hand a squeeze before moving off toward the door. "We'll see you downstairs, Bo."

"Okay. We'll be down shortly."

Sam stopped in the doorway, Adrian at his side, and looked back at Bo. Their gazes held for a moment. Sam tried to put as much reassurance as he could into his face. Bo's wan smile told him he'd been at least partially successful.

Turning away, Sam patted Adrian's back. "Come on, kiddo. Grab your bag and we'll get to work."

Adrian obediently hefted his stuffed duffle bag and trudged after Sam. Sam tried not to let his fear for the boy show on his face. Adrian knew he and everyone else was in danger as long as he stayed here. Learning how slim his chances of surviving a portal really were wouldn't help matters.

∞

Adrian fell asleep in the truck halfway to Sam and Bo's apartment. Bo carried him inside. Sam trailed behind with Adrian's duffle bag. He set it beside the bed while Bo pulled off Adrian's sneakers and tucked him under the covers. Bo pressed a gentle kiss to the boy's forehead before following Sam out of the room and closing the door.

They brushed their teeth and changed out of their clothes without speaking. Sam had to remind Bo to take his anti-seizure medication. Bo took the capsules without argument, but it worried Sam that he'd forgotten. He'd been taking them ever since his seizure back in May, and hadn't forgotten once until now.

When they switched off the light and climbed into bed, Bo still hadn't said a word. Worried by Bo's silence, Sam slipped his arm around Bo's waist and molded his body to Bo's back. "Are you all right?"

"No. I'm afraid, Sam." Bo turned to look at Sam. His eyes glittered black in the low light bleeding through the curtains. "He's safe tonight. But what about tomorrow night? And the night after that? What's going to happen to him and Sean, if we can't protect them?"

Sam's heart twisted. He tightened his arm around Bo. "We just have to take it one day at a time. Do the best we can."

Bo nodded, his hair tickling Sam's face. "I know you're right. It's just so tempting to take them and run. Just get them both the hell out of here before…"

He didn't finish the thought, but he didn't have to. Sam kissed the shell of Bo's ear. "You know we can't do that. It'll just put the kids in worse danger in the long run."

"I know." Bo drew a shaking breath. "God, I don't know what to do. I've never felt more helpless in my life."

A great fist seemed to close around Sam's chest. He wished he could take away the despair in Bo's voice.

"Try to sleep," Sam whispered in Bo's ear. "Things'll look better in the morning." It sounded false even to himself.

Bo let out a harsh laugh. "I can't sleep. Right now I feel like I'll never be able to sleep again."

With no idea what to say or do, Sam buried his face in Bo's neck and rubbed his hand in soothing circles on Bo's chest, as if he could erase Bo's fear with nothing but his touch.

Maybe you can, he thought when Bo's heartbeat quickened against his palm. *For a little while, at least.*

Sam trailed his fingers lower, over the threadbare cotton of Bo's T-shirt to the drawstring of the ancient hospital scrub pants he always wore to bed when he felt in need of comfort. A sharp tug loosened the bow. Sam slipped his hand inside and reached between Bo's legs, cupping his balls in his palm.

Bo moaned. "Sam. I don't know if—"

"Shhh." Sam nuzzled behind Bo's ear. He ran his fingertips over the head of Bo's cock, which began to swell in his hand. "Just relax. Let me touch you."

A tremor ran through Bo's body when Sam's fingers closed around his shaft and began to stroke. Hooking a thumb into the waistband of his scrubs, Bo shoved them down to mid-thigh. The drawstring dragged over Sam's prick where it pressed against Bo's ass. The thin material of Sam's boxers did not a damn thing to reduce the sensation.

Wanting to feel skin on skin but unwilling to let go of Bo's cock, Sam used the arm he was lying on to wriggle his boxers down as far as he could. When the garment was out of the way he squirmed until his erection lay nestled between Bo's buttocks. It felt wonderful, just as it always did. His cock fit perfectly in the warm, welcoming crease of Bo's ass, and his thighs molded to Bo's as if they were parts of one whole.

Bo's hand curved over Sam's on his cock. "Sam. Please."

Realizing he'd been lying there simply holding Bo for a couple of minutes now, Sam chuckled. "Sorry." He began stroking again, swiping the pad of his thumb across Bo's slit just to hear Bo's near-silent gasps when he did it.

Letting the movement of his hand fall into a rhythm so familiar it was second nature, Sam rooted into the thick tresses pooling around Bo's neck and breathed deep. Bo's hair always smelled so good, fresh and clean as a spring morning. The underlying musk of sexual desire added a familiar lusty kick, the two blending into the scent Sam loved more than any other.

Fastening his mouth to the juncture of Bo's neck and shoulder, Sam sucked the firm flesh. A hint of salt caressed his tastebuds. He pressed his tongue flat against Bo's skin to gather as much of the sharp flavor as he could.

Bo shivered, his body arching against Sam's. "Oh, God," he whispered, thrusting into Sam's hand. "Harder."

Electricity shot through Sam's insides. He obediently tightened his fingers around Bo's shaft and pulled harder, faster. Bo growled and pushed his ass against Sam's groin, and *fuck* but it felt good. Slipping his free hand beneath Bo's neck, Sam curled his arm around Bo's skull. His fingers dug into the silken warmth of Bo's hair and tugged Bo's head back, baring his neck for gentle open-mouthed kisses. Bo moaned, the sound low and sweet. His hips rocked, forward and backward and forward again, fucking Sam's hand and rubbing his ass against Sam's cock, until Sam was lost in a haze of heat and sensation.

For a while, the only sounds were their panting breaths and the faint squeak of the mattress with the movement of Sam's arm. Excitement spiraled tight in Sam's belly. There was something deliciously illicit about lying mostly dressed under the covers, humping against Bo's ass while he jerked Bo off.

Bo's breath hitched. His prick pulsed against Sam's palm. "Oh fuck. Sam. Close."

"That's it," Sam breathed, his fingers flying over Bo's cock. "Come in my hand."

A couple more hard tugs and Bo did, whimpering as his semen spurted onto his chest and coated Sam's hand. Twisting his head around, he met Sam's mouth in a deep kiss. The feel of Bo's tongue against his sent Sam tumbling over the edge. He came in a dizzying rush, his hand spasming around Bo's still-hard shaft. Slippery warmth seeped between his belly and Bo's back. He shut his eyes and let the swooping sensation pulse through him.

His lids dragged open again when Bo's lips pulled away

from his. He smiled at Bo's dazed expression. "Better now?"

"Mm-hm." Bo curled up and snuggled deeper into Sam's embrace. "Love you, Sam."

"Love you too." Reluctantly, Sam uncurled his fingers from Bo's softening cock. "Want to get cleaned up?"

All Sam got in answer was a grunt. He leaned over to look into Bo's face. Bo's eyelids drooped half shut. His expression was relaxed and drowsy. He gave Sam a vague smile before his eyes drifted closed.

Good. It worked.

Sam unwound his arms from around Bo, pulled off his T-shirt and swabbed the coagulating semen as best he could from Bo's chest, belly, groin and back. He wiped the spunk from his own abdomen, then tossed the garment onto the floor. After a few moments of careful work, Sam got Bo's scrub pants pulled back up and tied. Bo slept through the whole thing.

Sam shook his head. If all it took was a quick hand job to make Bo crash this hard, he must not have been sleeping well for a while now. It irked Sam that he hadn't noticed.

Yawning, Sam tugged his boxers back up before spooning once more against Bo's back. He snaked an arm around Bo's middle and rested his face against the back of Bo's neck.

The orgasm on top of the evening's events left him feeling exhausted. Sleep dragged at his mind. Closing his eyes, he gave himself up to its irresistible pull.

∞

When he woke, the clock read four thirty a.m. and Bo's side of the bed was empty. Sam pulled on a clean T-shirt and went looking for him.

He wasn't surprised to find Bo in Adrian's room, slouched in the single chair, watching his son sleep. Bo turned his head toward Sam when Sam entered the room. Even in the dark, Sam saw the forlorn look in Bo's eyes. Carefully avoiding the squeaky spots in the floor, Sam crossed to where Bo sat and held out his hand. Bo took it and let himself be pulled to his feet.

Knowing it was useless to take Bo back to bed right now, Sam led him into the living room and sat him down on the sofa. Sam switched on the TV, with the volume turned low. On screen, Humphrey Bogart wondered why, out of all the gin joints in all the world, Ingrid Bergman had to wander into his. The watery gray light from the mournful scene illuminated the dampness streaking Bo's cheeks.

Without a word, Sam wrapped both arms around Bo and pulled him close. Bo curled into his embrace, head resting in the curve of his neck and hands clutching his shirt with desperate strength.

Eventually, Bo's shoulders stopped shaking and the wetness dried from Sam's neck. Sam held his lover, cheek pressed to his hair and palms stroking his back, offering the only comfort he could.

Bo didn't sleep again until the first morning sunlight bled through the curtains. Sam sat there, deep in thought, and didn't sleep at all.

Chapter Eleven

Shadows swirled within shadows, hovering on the edge of solidity for a tantalizing second before dissipating again. The sleeve of a jacket lifted and pulled sideways toward a whorl of blackness nestled in the dark spaces between hanging garments, an open toy box, shelves of books and shoes. Clothes, books, even the folding closet doors seemed to bend inward like water circling a drain.

Frowning, Sam went back a few seconds in the video displayed on his computer monitor to replay the video of Adrian's closet once again. It was the video taken Friday night in Adrian's room, when he'd first seen the darkness coalesce like a living thing inside Adrian's closet.

He hadn't yet reached the part after he'd turned the light on and Adrian had lost his temper. The part when he'd felt the things beyond the dimensional barrier trying to force their way through. He told himself he hadn't moved on yet because he wanted to understand the first event before viewing the second, but the truth was both simpler and less palatable—he was afraid. Just plain fucking terrified to see what he knew he would see.

Berating himself for his cowardice, Sam hit "play" and prepared to watch the next few seconds for about the tenth time. He leaned forward and stared hard at the maelstrom on the screen. The heart of it seemed at first glance to be empty, but Sam knew it wasn't. Not really. The harder he looked, the more alive the blackness seemed to be. It moved. Pulsed. Reached inky pseudopods toward the dim golden glow of Adrian's nightlight.

When Sam's digital self jumped up to turn on the light, he stopped the video and pressed the heels of his hands to his forehead. He had no idea why the evidence from Friday night was affecting him more than the other cases. Maybe it was because Adrian was Bo's son, or because Sam had come to care for Adrian in his own right. Maybe it was because he hadn't seen actual video of a portal trying to open since Oleander House, and the memories of that time still tortured him in his nightmares. He didn't know. Whatever the reason, he didn't think he could keep watching. Not right now.

A hand gripped his shoulder. Sam turned and looked up into Dean's worried face. "You okay?" Dean asked.

"Yeah." Dean gave him a skeptical look, and Sam shook his head. "No. This video is freaking me out, to tell you the truth."

"Because it involves Adrian?"

"I don't know. But honestly, that's probably it."

Reaching behind him, Dean rolled Danny's chair over and plopped into it. "I can see that. So what've you found so far?"

Sam looked around the office, which was empty except for himself and Dean. Bo and Andre were closeted in Bo's office with the new client whose busy schedule was one reason they were here on a Saturday. The other reason waited in artificial stillness on his computer screen. Sam found the quiet depressing. He was glad Dean had offered to come in and help review the videos.

"Sam?"

Blinking, Sam turned back to Dean. "Sorry, what?"

"I was just asking what you've found on the video." With a quick glance toward Bo's closed office door, Dean rolled closer to Sam. "Although from the look on your face, I'd say the camera picked up the things you saw in Adrian's closet."

Sam nodded. "Yes. Or, well, it picked up what I saw first, before I turned on the light. I haven't watched any further than that yet." He didn't explain *why*, though Dean knew him well enough that he could probably guess. "What about you? Did the other camera catch anything?"

"As far as video, no, nothing." Dean's brow furrowed. "But there were some strange noises, after Adrian lost his temper."

"Right when the portal was trying to open, I bet." Groaning, Sam rubbed his eyes. "Shit. I guess I need to bite the bullet and watch the rest of my video."

"Well, it would be good to see if the sounds I heard correspond to anything on your tape." Dean jumped up and crossed to his computer, where he'd been watching the other video from Friday night. "I started hearing them at, hm, nine twenty-seven and twelve seconds. Right after Adrian threw that thing against the wall."

Swallowing his fear, Sam forwarded his video to nine twenty-seven and started it playing. Dean pulled his own chair over and sat beside Sam, leaning forward to watch the screen. Adrian's angry, wounded voice rose, his pajama-clad arm drifting in and out of view on the left side of the picture. Then came the crack of plastic shattering, followed by the hair-raising rasp that still made Sam want to run from the room as fast as he could.

In the video, nothing happened. Relief rushed through Sam's veins, leaving him weak. "It's not there." He glanced at Dean, a grin spreading over his face. "We must've—"

"You didn't." Dean pointed at the screen, eyes wide and

face white. "Look."

Sam forced himself to look. There on the video was the vortex-like thing he'd seen with his own eyes Friday night. He stared, frozen. Seeing it on video, knowing the impartial eye of the camera had recorded it as faithfully as everything else in the room, made it horribly real. He and Dean watched as the structure—*the portal,* Sam reminded himself, *call it what it is*—grew more solid over the next few seconds, tugging at the very air around it as if it were a black hole.

The light pulsed and waned. In the flickering illumination, Sam saw a hint of translucent obsidian reach through the widening portal. For a heartbeat, the room seemed to waver. Then the opening snapped shut and winked out of existence.

"This corresponds with the sounds on the other video, all right." Reaching across Sam, who hadn't moved, Dean stopped the video. He took Sam's hand and squeezed it. "You didn't let it open, Sam. You stopped it."

"What if I hadn't been there?" Sam searched Dean's eyes as if they held the answers to all his questions. "What happens next time, Dean? What happens when he's there alone, and he's afraid or angry?" An image of Amy's mutilated body flashed into his mind, her lifeless eyes fixed on him in silent accusation. He pulled his hand free of Dean's and rubbed his fingertips against his temples, as if he could erase the memory so easily. "I'm teaching him as much as I can, we worked together for nearly three hours this morning before Bo took him back to his mom's, but it's not *enough.* What if..."

He trailed off, fighting a surge of panic. *What if I can't protect him, and I can't teach him to protect himself? What if he ends up like those others—catatonic, a shell?*

What if he dies, like Amy did?

What if I fail again?

The thought was unbearable. Sam squeezed his eyes shut.

Hands grasped his shoulders and gave him a shake. "Sam. Look at me."

Sam opened his eyes. Dean's gaze bored into him with an intensity Sam rarely saw in his friend.

"You weren't responsible for Amy's death," Dean said, his voice gentle. "You did the best you could under truly horrible circumstances. Nobody can ask anything more of you than your best."

"This is different."

"Yes, it is. You have even less control over what happens this time." Dean laid one open palm on Sam's cheek. "You're doing everything you can, Sam. Nobody expects you to be Superman. You have to stop expecting that of yourself."

Sam's throat constricted. Hooking an arm around Dean's neck, Sam pulled him into a tight hug. "Thank you. For everything." The words were inadequate to express the depth of Sam's gratitude for Dean's friendship and support over the past year, but Sam figured Dean understood.

Dean's arm wound around Sam's back, returning the hug. As they drew apart, the front door squeaked open. Sam plastered on the best smile he could muster and prepared to greet whoever had just come in.

His smile froze on his face when he met a pair of icy hazel eyes. He glanced sideways, saw that Dean had minimized the damning video on his computer screen and breathed a sigh of relief. "Janine." Moving as surreptitiously as he could, he shut down his own video before Janine could see.

"Sam." Crossing her arms, she aimed a gloating look at Sam. "Did I interrupt something?"

Sam's mouth dropped open when he realized what she

meant. "Of course not."

"Really? Y'all looked pretty cozy to me." She shook her head. "Of course, I've heard you people are promiscuous. I just hope Bo knows what he's gotten himself into. Or does he join in?"

You people? Fury boiled up in Sam's gut. Standing, he planted both palms flat on Danny's desk and fixed Janine with a hard glare. "What you just saw was me hugging one of my closest friends. That's all. I love Bo more than anything in this life. I have never—*never*—been unfaithful to him, and I never will be." The memory of what David had told him nearly a year ago suddenly came back to him. He gave Janine an evil grin. "Which is more than you can say, isn't it?"

The instant the words were out, Sam knew he'd gone too far. He winced.

Janine's face went gray. She opened her mouth as if she was going to respond, then snapped it shut again when Bo's office door opened. She spun to face him, her expression shuttered. "Hello, Bo."

"Oh. Hi, Janine." Bo shot a wary glance between Janine, Sam and Dean, who sat watching the drama in silence. "What're you doing here?"

"You weren't at home. I know how often you work on weekends, so I took a chance." Her eyes, narrowed to slits, cut sideways at Sam, then back to Bo. "I have to talk to you. In private."

Andre emerged from the office. An elderly woman in an expensive-looking linen suit walked beside him. He cleared his throat, obviously warning the rest of them to be on their best behavior in the presence of a customer. "All right, Ms. Osbourne. We'll be in touch in the next few days."

"Thank you very much, Mr. Meloy." She shook Andre's

hand, then Bo's. "Dr. Broussard. Thank you for accommodating my schedule. I realize this isn't a usual workday for you."

"It's no trouble at all." Bo flashed her the bright smile which always charmed men and women alike. "Please call us if anything else happens, or if you have any questions."

With a brisk nod and a curious glance at Janine, Ms. Osbourne strode across the floor with a clack of heels on wood and exited into the waning late-afternoon sun.

Bo let out a deep breath. "Okay. Janine, come on in my office and we'll talk."

"Thank you." Head held high, Janine followed Bo into his office. The glare she darted at Sam on the way was sharp enough to gut anyone who gave a damn what she thought.

Sam liked to think he wasn't one of those people. Unfortunately, a small part of him mourned the loss of the tentative truce they'd been so close to forming not long ago.

Of course, it didn't help matters that he'd given in to temptation and prodded her with his knowledge of her past infidelity. It had felt good, but he might've just destroyed whatever miniscule chance he and Bo may have had of making peace with the woman. Sighing, he fell back into his chair and stared morosely into space.

"Well. Okay, that was interesting. I'm heading home now." Andre snagged his jacket off the coat rack. He glanced at Bo's office door. "Try not to have a massacre, huh?"

"Yeah, well, it won't be my fault," Sam muttered as Andre left. "Dammit, I can't believe she said that."

Dean's eyebrows shot up. "Seriously? Uh, we *are* talking about Janine here, right? The Wicked Bitch of the South? The woman who has insulted you and cut you down at every possible opportunity ever since she found out about you and Bo?"

156

"I know, I know. It's just that lately, sometimes, it seemed like she was trying to get along. I *liked* that, and not just for Bo's sake. I'm so fucking tired of fighting with her. I'm tired of always feeling like I'm walking on broken glass when she's around." Sam ran a frustrated hand through his hair. "This is the worst possible time for us to be at each other's throats. If Janine and I could get along, even a little bit, maybe she'd be more willing to let Adrian spend more time with Bo and me." *Where he's safe.*

"Yeah, maybe. But she was pretty shitty to Bo even before she knew about the two of you, so I'm thinking she wouldn't change her mind about y'all keeping the boys more often anyway."

Sam had to admit Dean was probably right. He scowled, frustrated. He hated feeling so powerless.

Bo's office door swung open. Janine marched through, mouth tight and gaze downcast. She shot a swift glance at Sam as she yanked open the outside door and left the building. Sam frowned, wondering if he'd imagined the flash of remorse in her eyes.

Dean caught Sam's eye. He shook his head. He didn't any more know what Janine had said than Dean did.

Bo shuffled out of his office, walked around Danny's desk and plopped into her chair. He stared into space, chewing on one thumbnail.

Concerned by the stunned look on Bo's face, Sam rolled his chair closer. "Bo? What happened?"

Bo blinked and focused on Sam's face. "She's bringing the boys over early for their weekend with us. Wednesday, after school. And she wants them to stay with us Sunday night too. We're supposed to bring them back to her place Monday evening."

Relief and puzzlement warred for space in Sam's mind. Puzzlement won. "That's great, but why?"

"Adrian. Apparently he's been on her case to let him live with us."

Sam's pulse faltered. He wanted Adrian to be safe, but he wasn't sure he was ready to have the boy around all the time. Adrian wasn't the easiest child in the world to deal with, and the tension between them hadn't abated entirely, even though Adrian had thawed a great deal toward Sam in the past few weeks.

"Don't tell me he actually wore her down," Dean chimed in, leaning forward in his chair.

"Not exactly. But she's going out of town again, for several days this time, and decided it would be easier for everyone if she let the boys stay with us while she's gone." Bo let out a harsh laugh. "Apparently Adrian's been having daily hysterics, begging her to let him come live with us. He hasn't been sleeping, and he's been neglecting his schoolwork."

"Hm." Dean rubbed the back of his neck, his expression thoughtful. "Sounds like she wants to do what's best for Adrian and is just hiding behind the going-out-of-town excuse."

"That could be," Bo agreed. "As much as she irritates me, and as many hateful things as she's said to Sam and me, she's always been a good mother to the boys."

Sam took Bo's hand in his. "He didn't tell her *why* he wants to live with us, did he?"

Bo shook his head. "No, thank God. I don't think she would've given in even this far if he had."

"Maybe this means she's finally getting used to the idea of you and Sam being together," Dean speculated.

"Maybe." Sam turned Bo's hand over and traced his lifeline

with one finger. "It seems unlikely, though, considering what she said before."

Bo frowned. "What do you mean?"

Sam and Dean glanced at each other. "She walked into the office right when I was giving Dean a hug," Sam explained. "She kind of got the wrong idea."

A tangle of emotions—hurt, jealousy, anger—flashed through Bo's eyes and was gone before Sam could decide what it meant. One dark brow arched in amusement. "Maybe she really is evolving. She didn't say a thing to me, and I know she wouldn't normally pass up the opportunity to put you down."

Guilt pricked Sam's conscience. He knew damn well why Janine hadn't said anything—fear of retribution in kind. Did the fact that he was dying to tell Bo about Janine's cheating past make him just as bad as her? Or did his continued silence on the subject make him even worse?

It's in the past, he reminded himself. *It doesn't matter anymore either way. Just forget it.*

Shoving the whole issue to the back of his mind, Sam pinned Bo with a searching look. "She *did* get the wrong idea. You know that, right?" Sam knew the answer—or at least he hoped he did—but he needed to hear it from Bo. Otherwise he'd never be able to forget the fleeting uncertainty in Bo's eyes which said maybe he wasn't quite as okay with Sam and Dean's one-night sexual history as they'd both thought.

Bo stared straight into Sam's eyes, his own wide open and unshuttered. "Yes, Sam. I know she did." *I trust you,* his slight smile seemed to say.

Relieved, Sam nodded. "I just wanted to make sure."

He could feel Dean watching them both. Dean never said so, but Sam knew he still felt guilty about their one night together almost a year ago, even though Sam and Bo had been broken up at the time.

Leaning forward, Bo planted a soft kiss on Sam's lips. "What have y'all found on the videos from Friday?"

"The camera caught what Sam and Adrian saw in the closet," Dean answered, obviously glad for the change of subject. "The other camera caught the sounds, but didn't show anything on video."

Renewed worry clouded Bo's eyes. "So it was real. I was afraid of that."

"Adrian will be with us for five nights. I'll have lots of time to work with him on perfecting his control." Sam picked up the braid falling over Bo's shoulder and let it run like a living rope across his palm. "What happened was real, yes. But we'll deal with it. We'll help Adrian deal with it. It'll be okay."

Bo nodded. "Yeah. Of course it will."

Something told Sam that Bo didn't believe that any more than he did.

∞

Sam's feet thudded on the sidewalk. His lungs drew in biting winter air and blew out white fog with each harsh breath.

It was too cold for an outdoor run, really. Twenty-nine degrees, with a damp, cutting wind rolling off the Bay. But Sam didn't care. Jogging along in the frigid early morning cleared his head and released some of the tension which had been building inside him for days on end. At just after dawn on a Sunday, the waterfront streets were eerily deserted, and Sam relished having the stately old buildings and gnarled, ancient oaks to himself.

Normally, Bo would've been right there with him. Morning runs together had become a routine for them. The last few days, though, Sam had been forced to go alone since Bo refused to leave the boys by themselves even for an hour.

Sam was acutely aware of the empty space beside him, but at the same time he enjoyed the solitude. He was glad Sean and Adrian were out of Janine's house, even if it was only temporary. Having them around under this particular set of circumstances, however, was proving to be more stressful than he'd anticipated. He'd worked with Adrian for at least a couple of hours every day, and the boy had already made huge strides in his control techniques, but his fear of returning to his mother's house hadn't abated one bit. A frightened Adrian meant a sullen and argumentative Adrian, which in turn meant an equally frightened—and extremely short-tempered—Bo.

Sam couldn't blame Bo for being in a bad mood. But that didn't make it any easier to deal with.

The miles passed in a blur of cracked concrete and bare winter branches, and before Sam knew it he was slowing to a walk in front of the building where Bo and the children waited. Digging his keys out of the pocket of his sweatpants, he unlocked the front door and climbed the stairs to their apartment. Part of him hoped Bo and the kids would still be asleep. Another part of him hated the fact that he felt that way.

The apartment was as dark and silent as it had been when Sam left over an hour before. He eased the deadbolt into place, set his keys on the counter and headed for the bedroom as quietly as possible.

In the watery morning light coming through the curtains, he could just make out the shape of Bo's body curled beneath the covers. Toeing off his running shoes, Sam padded over to the bed and stood gazing down at the one person he'd ever loved with his whole being. Bo's face was slack and peaceful in sleep, the lines of fear and worry smoothed away.

Sam bent and pressed a gentle kiss to Bo's temple. Bo didn't stir. Trying to pretend he hadn't hoped for Bo to wake up and drag him into bed, Sam dug clean clothes out of his dresser drawer and went to the bathroom to take a shower.

He emerged to the scent of coffee brewing. Smiling, he wandered down the hallway and into the kitchen. He sidled up behind Bo, who stood gazing into the open refrigerator, slid both arms around his waist and kissed the side of his neck. "Good morning, gorgeous."

"Good morning." Bo turned his head to kiss Sam's lips. "How was your run?"

"Cold."

"Yes, funny how that happens in November." Leaning forward, Bo grabbed the eggs and milk, set them on the counter and kicked the refrigerator door shut. He twisted around with a smile and pressed his body against Sam's, both arms going around Sam's neck. "You should've stayed in bed, where it's warm."

The seductive purr in Bo's voice went straight to Sam's crotch, much to his chagrin. He and Bo hadn't had sex in over a week, and Sam knew damn well it wasn't going to happen now. He didn't think it would happen even if they weren't currently in the kitchen, with the boys only a few yards away and likely to wake up at any moment. Bo simply hadn't been in the mood lately. Not that Sam blamed him, but this teasing when they both knew nothing would come of it was irritating, to say the least.

Since when is it "teasing" when he touches you, or kisses you? Sam snorted. Apparently lack of regular sex did funny things to his perceptions. It was an uncomfortable thing to discover about oneself, and he didn't much like it.

"Sam?" Bo nuzzled under Sam's chin, his tongue flicking

over the freshly shaved skin. "What's wrong?"

Unable to articulate his frustration—sexual and otherwise—Sam crushed Bo close and took his mouth in a hard, rough kiss.

Bo instantly went boneless in Sam's arms. His mouth opened, and for a while nothing existed for Sam but teeth and tongues and the bruising grip of Bo's fingers in his hair and on the back of his neck. He rocked his hips, just to hear Bo's helpless little moan when their cocks rubbed against each other through sweats and scrub pants.

"Ewwww, gross! Stop it!"

They jumped apart. Heart racing, Sam stared at Sean, who stood in the foyer with both small hands over his eyes. Bare feet poked out from beneath the hems of his Halo pajamas.

Sam let out a breathless laugh. He felt like he was in a scene from a sitcom. At least he and Bo hadn't been going at it long enough for him to be hard.

Bo leveled a glowering look at his son. "Sean, what have I told you about saying things like that?"

Sean dropped his hands and clasped them behind his back. "That grownups can kiss all they want in their own house." He gave them a sheepish smile. "Sorry."

Shaking his head, Bo took the eggs and milk he'd gotten out a few minutes before and carried them to the stove. "Is your brother up?"

"Yeah. He's getting dressed." Sean yawned, one hand scratching his sleep-tousled head. "What're you making, Dad?"

"Pancakes." Bo shot Sean a knowing grin. "I hope that's okay. I can make oatmeal or poached eggs if you'd rather."

"No!" Laughing, Sean ran into the kitchen and gave his father a rib-cracking hug. "I want pancakes."

Bo chuckled. "Okay. Pancakes it is." Leaning down, Bo kissed the top of Sean's head. "Set the table for me. It'll be ready in a few minutes."

"'Kay."

Sam watched Sean stand on tiptoe to lift four plates from the cabinet, then carry them carefully to the table. "You know, he's such a good kid, I can't even be mad at him for interrupting," Sam murmured in Bo's ear.

Bo shot him an amused look colored with annoyance. "That's very big of you. Thanks."

Sighing, Sam pulled away. "It *has* been a while, Bo."

"Nine days, more or less." Bo opened the cabinet and fished out a large mixing bowl. "Hardly forever."

"It is when you're used to nearly every day."

Bo cracked an egg against the side of the bowl so hard the shell shattered. "I know damn well you're not in this relationship just for the sex, Sam. So why are you being this way?"

The unmistakable hurt in Bo's voice made Sam feel like a heel. He leaned against the counter, watching Bo's face. "You're right. I'm sorry. I'm not really mad or anything, I completely understand why you haven't been in the mood. Hell, I haven't either, really." He shrugged. "I guess I'm just kind stressed out right now."

Bo's expression softened. "I guess we both are." Leaning forward, he kissed Sam's chin, then his lips. "Sam, I—"

Whatever he'd been about to say was cut short by an outraged wail from Sean. "No! Give it here, Adrian!"

Sam looked up, startled. He hadn't even noticed Adrian's presence.

"Shit." With a grimace, Bo set down the empty eggshell he

still held and hurried into the living room with Sam at his heels. "Okay, what's going on?"

"I was watching SpongeBob, and he turned the channel." Sean let go of the remote he'd been trying to wrestle from his brother, jumped up from the sofa and turned to Bo with pure outrage on his face. "Make him turn it back, Dad."

Adrian rolled his eyes, the picture of preteen disdain. "SpongeBob's stupid. I want to watch the show about giant squids on the Discovery Channel."

Spinning around, Sean aimed a murderous look at his brother. "I don't care, I was watching SpongeBob first!"

"Well, then you're stupid too."

Bo caught Sean's arm to keep him from lunging at Adrian. "Okay, that's enough. Adrian, turn the channel back."

Adrian's eyes went wide. "But, Dad, I really wanted to watch this show."

"You can watch it in your room."

"The picture on that TV sucks."

"I'm sorry, son, but your brother was already watching SpongeBob." He glanced at Sam. "You can use the TV in our room if you'd rather."

"That picture sucks too!"

Bo let out a sigh. "Adrian. Turn the channel back and go watch your show somewhere else."

Adrian's mouth tightened, making him look a lot like his mother for a moment. "Fine." He switched the channel, slammed the remote onto the table and shoved to his feet. "There's your *stupid* cartoon, you big baby."

Sean glared at Adrian's back as he stomped off. "Weirdo."

Adrian stopped and turned on his heel, dark eyes snapping. "Shut *up!*"

165

"Make me!"

Something shifted in the pit of Sam's stomach. He heard Bo admonishing the boys to stop fighting, heard Sean arguing that it wasn't his fault, but their voices were drowned out in a swell of crackling energy. Adrian's eyes widened, clearly realizing what was about to happen, but it was too late. The energy burst like an invisible bomb. The TV flickered and went off. The overhead light exploded. In the sudden gloom, Sam heard the tinkle of glass hitting the wood floor.

"Dad?" Sean called, his voice high and frightened. "What happened?"

"It, um, must've been a power surge or something." Glass crunched under Bo's slippers as he crossed the room. "Sean, don't move yet, I don't want you to step on the broken glass and cut your feet."

The TV turned itself back on just as Bo switched on the lamp. The renewed light revealed glittering glass shards covering the living room floor. Most had landed on the bare wood, missing the furniture and the throw rug underneath it. Sean, still standing beside the sofa, seemed to be in the clear. With a quick look to make sure it was safe, Sean climbed back onto the sofa and curled up in the corner, hazel eyes huge.

"Adrian?" Bo walked over to where Adrian stood stiff as a post at the entrance to the hallway, his eyes screwed shut. "Son, are you okay?"

The boy didn't answer. Moving closer, Sam saw the deep, even, in-and-out of his breathing, just a little too fast. "You're doing your breathing," Sam said, keeping his voice low and soothing. "That's good. You're doing really well."

Bo shot an agonized glance at Sam, and Sam knew Bo had already deduced that what just happened hadn't been a power surge. "It's over now, Adrian. It's okay." Kneeling carefully on the floor in front of Adrian, Bo cupped Adrian's face in his hands. "Adrian. Open your eyes now, sweetheart. It's okay."

One brown eye cracked open, then the other. Both glittered with a fear just short of panic. "I'm sorry, Dad. I didn't mean to."

"I know, son." Bo managed a smile, though Sam could tell it was forced. "It's all right. Nothing that can't be fixed."

"But I lost control," Adrian whispered. "It was just Sean being a little jerk, and it made me..." His gaze cut to the broken light. "It made me do *that*. What am I gonna do when we're back in the other house? What if I get mad again?"

Bo hesitated, chewing his lower lip and looking more lost than Sam had ever seen him. His silence lasted just long enough for Adrian to draw his own conclusions.

Shoving Bo's hands away, Adrian backed up, looking stricken. "You think I'll make *that thing* come out, don't you?"

Bo stood, shaking his head. "Listen to me. Everything's going to be okay. This was just one little incident. It doesn't mean anything bad's going to happen at your mom's house."

The words were spoken with confidence, but the truth showed in Bo's eyes, and Sam knew Adrian saw it. Without a word, Adrian spun around and ran into his and Sean's room, slamming the door behind him.

"Shit." Bo rubbed a hand across his forehead. "Now what?"

Sam looped an arm around Bo's shoulders, leaned in and kissed his brow. "You want me to go talk to him?"

"No, I'll do it." Bo gave him a wan smile. "I think he could use another session with you later on, though, after he calms down."

"Of course. We were planning to practice some visualization today anyhow. He's been doing extremely well on learning control. I'm actually kind of surprised this happened."

Sean's uncharacteristically subdued voice broke into their murmured conversation. "Hey, Dad? Is Adrian all right?"

Bo walked over to his youngest son and kissed the top of his head. "He'll be fine. I'm just going to go talk to him for a minute, then I'll be back to make breakfast, okay?"

"'Kay." Sean sat up on his knees to peer over the back of the sofa as Bo headed toward the boys' bedroom. "Me and Sam can clean up the glass while you're talking to Adrian."

"That's a very good idea," Bo agreed. "Just make sure you put on some shoes first."

Bo caught Sam's hand and squeezed it on the way to Sean and Adrian's room. Sam squeezed back, giving as much encouragement as he could. Squaring his shoulders, Bo tapped on the bedroom door, turned the knob and swung it open.

Once Bo shut the door behind him, Sam turned back to Sean with a smile. "Okay. Let's get this mess cleaned up. You want to vacuum?"

Sean's eyes lit up, and Sam chuckled. For reasons Sam couldn't quite fathom, Sean loved to vacuum.

"Yeah." Sean pointed to the pile of assorted footwear beside the front door. "My school shoes are there."

Sam grabbed the shoes from the pile and handed them to Sean. Struck with a sudden thought, he sat beside the boy while he pulled on his shoes. "Sean? Don't say anything to your mom about this, okay?"

Sean blinked at Sam, surprise in his eyes. "How come?"

How come indeed? Not knowing how to explain without telling Sean things he probably wouldn't want to hear, Sam settled on a partial truth. "She wouldn't like what happened. She might not think it's safe for you and Adrian to stay with us anymore."

Sean's eyes widened. "I won't tell her."

"Great. Thanks."

Sam pushed to his feet and headed for the hall closet to fetch the vacuum. Sean followed him like an eager puppy. Fishing the vacuum out of the closet, Sam let Sean roll it into the living room. He watched with an indulgent smile while Sean plugged in the machine and started cleaning up the glass littering the floor. The sight of Sean singing the SpongeBob theme song while he worked brought a surge of fierce protectiveness through Sam's chest.

Please, let Bo and me be able to keep them safe. Please.

Sam wished he could believe someone was listening.

∞

Sunday passed without further incident. Sam and Bo dropped the children at their school Monday morning and left, hoping for the best. Nine days passed with no word from Janine, Lee or either of the boys. Bo did his best to keep up the illusion of normality, but Sam could tell how worried he was. Nearly every night, Sam woke in the small hours to find Bo curled on the sofa reading or watching TV. He never tried to push Bo to talk, just settled beside him and held him until he dozed off again.

By the day before Thanksgiving, Sam was exhausted from worry and lack of sleep, and he knew Bo felt even worse. Stifling a yawn, Sam saved the report from their last case and hit print. It was the last of the work before they shut down for the holiday. Normally they worked the day after Thanksgiving. Sam didn't mind, since he didn't spend time with his mother or sister, but this time he was glad Bo had decided not to open on Friday. His eyes felt gritty, his lids lead-weighted. He'd never been more ready for a break in his life.

Something nudged his arm. He looked up to meet Cecile's concerned gaze. "Here," she said, holding out a steaming mug full of coffee that smelled like pumpkin pie spice. "Thought you could use some caffeine."

He took the mug with a grateful smile. "You thought right. Thanks." He blew on the hot liquid and took a sip. "Mm. Good."

She patted his shoulder. "You look worn out."

"Almost as worn out as Bo." Danny swiveled around to arch an eyebrow at him. "I do hope the two of you are planning to relax over the next few days."

"Yeah, it's just..." Sam trailed off, tracing the rim of his mug with his thumb. They hadn't told anyone at the office about the latest incident with Adrian, and Sam had no idea how to explain how much stress he and Bo were under without that fairly vital piece of information.

"The kids," Andre guessed, emerging from the back room. "Bo's worried about the kids, isn't he? Since their house is showing potential for portal formation."

"Yeah, exactly." Sam glanced toward Bo's office, where Bo was holed up finishing some financial spreadsheet or other. "I think Bo's only doing the accounting to distract him from thinking about the boys and what might be happening there."

David laughed. "No way. He's way too much of a control freak to let go of the money stuff, even though we all know Danny would be better at it."

"Thank you," Danny said, smiling. "But I believe Bo manages quite well."

Closing the PhotoShop document he'd been working on for

the BCPI website, Dean spun around in his chair. "Has anything else happened at the house since we were out there?"

"Not that we know of. But of course Janine doesn't talk to us if she doesn't have to, so who knows. Though I think Lee would've called if anything major happened." Sam didn't mention Bo's belief that even though Lee might call if he knew something had happened, Adrian was just as likely to keep any events to himself as to tell Lee.

Cecile frowned. "Maybe this is a silly question, but if nothing's happened, why is Bo so worried? He looks like he hasn't slept for a week, and frankly, Sam, you don't look much better. Is something else going on?"

Sam hesitated, unsure of how to answer. He took a swallow of coffee. "Well—"

Before he could continue, the front door swung open and a petite woman in a mail carrier's uniform walked in. Sam smiled at her. "Hi, Kathryn."

"Hi, Sam." She looked around. "Where's Bo? I have a certified letter for him. He needs to sign for it."

"He's in his office." Danny stood and started to Bo's door. "I'll get him for you."

"Great, thanks."

Danny knocked on Bo's door. "Bo, can you come out here for a moment? You need to sign for a certified letter."

The door swung open. Walking out, he approached the mail carrier with a strained smile. He scribbled his name on the form and took the letter. "Thanks, Kathryn."

"Sure. See y'all." She left with a wave, the door squeaking shut behind her.

Bo glanced at the envelope. A scowl twisted his features. "Shit. It's from Janine's lawyer."

Cecile gasped. "What? Why would he be sending you a certified letter?"

"I don't know." Bo snatched the letter opener from Danny's desk and slit open the envelope.

Setting down his coffee, Sam walked around to stand beside Bo as he pulled out the single sheet of paper. "What's it say?"

Bo scanned the paper, and all the color drained from his face. "Fuck. Oh, fuck. No."

Alarmed, Sam slipped his arm around Bo's waist. "What? What is it?"

Bo turned to Sam, his face gray with shock. "Janine's trying to take away my visitation."

Chapter Twelve

Sam snatched the paper out of Bo's unresisting hand. Four paragraphs of stilted legalese boiled down to what Bo had already said—Janine had petitioned the court for a new custody hearing, in order to take away Bo's visitation with his sons.

"She can't do this." Sam dropped the letter on Danny's desk and laid both hands on Bo's face. "We're going to fight this, do you hear me? She has no right to keep you from seeing your kids. We won't let her."

"Damn right we won't." To Sam's relief, some of the color returned to Bo's cheeks. Fire filled his hollow eyes for the first time in days. "Stay here. I'll be back."

Brushing past Sam, Bo strode over to the coat rack. Sam followed, apprehension curling in his gut. "Bo? Where are you going?"

"Out." Bo snatched his jacket off the rack and pulled it on. He glanced at the clock on the wall. "Folks, it's nearly four o'clock. We're now officially closed for Thanksgiving. Y'all go on home."

Everyone looked at each other as if they wanted to say something, but didn't know what. Andre shook his head. "I don't think you should do this when you're mad."

"Duly noted." Snatching the letter off Danny's desk, Bo yanked open the front door and stalked out without another word.

With a quick glance at the shocked faces of his coworkers, Sam followed. He caught Bo just as he reached his car. "Bo, Andre's right. This is a bad idea."

"No, Sam, I don't think it is." Bo took his keys out of his jacket pocket and opened the car door. "Don't worry, I'm not going over there to get in a screaming match. I want to talk to her, that's all."

"You know as well as I do that it won't work out that way. If you don't start a fight, she will." Sam grabbed Bo's arm. "Bo, please, don't."

The muscle in Bo's jaw twitched. "Let go."

"Bo—"

Bo shook him off, brown eyes blazing. "What court do you think is going to take my side over Janine's if she tells them we're teaching Adrian about psychic powers and monsters from another dimension? I have to stop this *now*, before it gets that far, or I might not ever see my children again."

Sam had no answer for that. "Let me come with you."

Bo gave him an incredulous look. "Oh yes, because you being around just calms her right down."

"You're going to her office, right? I'll stay in the waiting room."

"No."

Moving closer, Sam rested a hand on Bo's hip. "I just don't want you to have to face this alone, Bo. Please, let me come. I swear I'll stay out of sight. I'll even wait in the car if you want."

Bo didn't move or speak, but Sam could see his surrender in the way his shoulders slumped. Sam waited. After a few moments, Bo sighed and slid behind the wheel. "Fine. Come with me, and wait in the car."

It wasn't perfect, but it was good enough. At least Sam would have the illusion of doing something useful if he went with Bo. If he stayed at the BCPI office, he'd go crazy.

Sam ran to the other side of the car, opened the door and climbed in. Filing the letter in the glove compartment, Bo cranked the engine and pulled out into the afternoon traffic.

Fifteen minutes later, Bo guided the car into the small parking lot behind the office of the magazine where Janine worked. He parked, undid his seatbelt and turned to Sam. "Promise me you'll stay right here."

"I will," Sam said, fighting the urge to insist on going with him.

They stared at each other. Sam wished he had something wise and profound to say, but he didn't. So he sat gazing into Bo's eyes and trying to communicate telepathically all the half-formed thoughts in his head.

Bo lunged forward and kissed Sam hard, then jumped out of the car. Sam leaned back in his seat and shut his eyes, steeling himself for a long, tense wait.

When Bo emerged less than two minutes later, Sam didn't know whether to be relieved or afraid. He didn't think Janine had changed her mind that easily, which meant either she'd set a time to talk to Bo later—which Sam found almost as unlikely as her changing her mind—or she'd thrown him out without seeing him. Sam watched Bo's face as he approached, but his expression was unrevealing.

"What happened?" Sam demanded as soon as Bo opened the door.

"She wasn't there." Bo got in, buckled up and started the engine. "She's taking the day off."

"So she's at home." Sam studied Bo's profile, half afraid to ask. "Are you—?"

"Yes. I'm going over there." Twisting around, Bo backed out of his parking space. "I'll take you back to the office first."

"No, you will not." Sam grabbed the strap over his door as Bo peeled out of the parking lot. "Maybe I should drive."

The glower Bo gave Sam in response was answer enough. Sighing, Sam slumped in his seat. "I'm coming in with you."

"No, you're not. You're staying in the car."

Bo swerved across all three lanes of traffic, setting off a cacophony of horns. Sam swallowed his heart back down. "You're way too angry to confront Janine alone right now. You'll just make it worse."

"Fuck," Bo swore, swerving again to avoid the ancient Cadillac which had pulled out in front of him and immediately stopped. "Dammit, Sam, don't lecture me. I know what I'm doing."

Closing his eyes, Sam counted to fifteen. He opened his eyes again and aimed the calmest look he could manage at the side of Bo's head. "I know you, Bo. You're always calmer at first, then you start getting mad and it just escalates. You had your calm period at the office. Now you're getting seriously pissed off, and you know how you are when you get like that."

Bo shot him a glare, but didn't argue. Encouraged, Sam plowed on. "If I thought I could talk you out of seeing Janine right now altogether, I would. I know that's not going to happen. But I am *not* letting you go in there alone and screw things up for good. I'm going with you to keep you in line."

"This is a family matter," Bo snapped. "You don't need to be involved."

Now *that* hurt. Swallowing the urge to lash out, Sam forced himself to answer without rancor. "You and I love each other, Bo. We're committed to each other. That makes us family. I'm not letting you leave me behind when I know damn well you need me there."

Some of the fury faded from Bo's face. He darted Sam a glance that tried to be angry and annoyed but looked more guilty than anything else. "Fine."

He didn't speak again, but he'd evidently given up on fighting Sam's decision. Sam counted that as a victory.

By the time Bo pulled into Janine and Lee's driveway, he seemed a little calmer. Sam was glad of that, but he was still determined to be at Bo's side during the coming confrontation. To his relief, Bo didn't try to talk him out of it again. They got out of the car and approached the front door hand in hand.

Bo had to ring the doorbell twice before anyone answered. Sam heard raised voices before the door swung open to reveal Janine standing there in ratty sweats, looking like she hadn't had any more sleep in the past few days than Bo had.

Her eyes narrowed. "What the hell are you two doing here?"

"I got the letter from your lawyer today," Bo said. "I'd like to discuss this with you."

His voice was steady, but his hand shook in Sam's. Sam gave his fingers a reassuring squeeze.

"There's nothing to talk about. Now please get off my property."

Bo caught the door when Janine tried to swing it shut. "Janine, please. I don't understand why you're doing this."

"Seriously?" Shaking her head, she barked a sharp laugh. "You know what, the fact that you don't understand is a huge part of the problem."

Sam took one look at the redness climbing Bo's neck and decided to intervene. "Can you explain it to us?"

She shot Sam a look full of nearly palpable hatred. "You're *psychic*, aren't you? Why don't you just read my fucking mind?"

The fingers of Sam's free hand balled into a fist. He shoved it in his pocket before he could give in to the temptation to use it. "It doesn't work that way."

Bo let out an impatient huff. "Just tell us what we've done this time."

She crossed her arms. "I warned you that I'd take this step if you kept filling the boys' heads with these crazy ideas about portals and monsters. You didn't listen. Now you're paying the price."

Sam's stomach dropped into his feet. *Oh shit.* He glanced at Bo, who had gone an unhealthy shade of gray.

Bo's fingers tightened around Sam's to the point of pain. "I don't know what you're talking about."

If Sam hadn't already known Bo was lying, he didn't think he'd have been able to tell. Janine, however, wasn't buying it. She gave them a cold smile. "Never say anything in front of Sean unless you want everyone to know about it."

Bo swayed and leaned against Sam's shoulder. "Janine, please. You can't take them away from me. I'm their father. They *need* me."

Janine stalked out onto the porch, eyes snapping. "What they *need*, you arrogant prick, is to be free of all the bullshit you've been feeding them." She pointed behind her, into the empty foyer. "Adrian is terrified of sleeping in his own room. Sean runs away crying every time Adrian gets the least bit angry. Why do you think that is, huh? Because they weren't like that until you two *sick fucks* put these insane ideas in their heads."

"There's no need for name-calling." Sam gave himself a mental pat on the back for managing to sound calm in spite of his rising anger.

"Sick. Fucks," she repeated, stabbing a finger at each of

them in turn. "If you think it's easy for me to tell my sons they can't see their father anymore, you are sadly mistaken. I don't want to do this. You two are forcing my hand."

Bo stared at her. Sam could practically see the wheels turning in his head, trying to find a way out of the mess they'd found themselves in. "Come to the office," Bo said. "I'll show you the vid—"

He stopped, eyes widening in realization of what he'd almost said. Sam bit his lip. He couldn't meet Janine's gaze.

"The video you took here, in *my* house, while I was gone?" she finished for him. "The video you tried to keep secret from me? Yes, Adrian told me you were here, when he was begging me once again to go live with you. I don't need to see your video to know there are no monsters in my home other than the ones you've planted in my children's imaginations."

An idea struck Sam, and he went with it. "Did you talk to Lee about this? He was here. He knows that what happened was real."

"Yes, I've talked to Lee." She spat the name like it was poisonous. "You'll excuse me if I don't give anything he says too much credence right now."

Her gaze met Sam's for a moment. She looked away quickly, but not before Sam saw the hurt in her eyes. He couldn't find it in him to feel sorry for her, but he felt a stab of guilt for having put Lee in the position of betraying Janine's trust. Lee had been a huge help to them, and thus to Adrian, and didn't deserve whatever hell Janine had probably put him through in the past few days.

"Lee was only trying to help," Bo told her. "Don't take it out on him."

"Oh yeah, I'm really going to take relationship advice from a man who strung me along for *years*, then ran off to shack up with some slut. Serves you right that he's fucking around behind your back, after what you did to me." Janine's gaze cut to Sam. Her eyes glittered with malice. "I caught him making out with that pretty boy in your office, right there out front where anyone could see."

It didn't matter that Bo already knew precisely what Janine had seen, what it was and what it wasn't. The fury which had been simmering in Sam's chest boiled over. "Hey, if you call a hug between friends 'making out', what would you call it when a wife propositions her husband's friends for sex?" He couldn't help the smirk that spread across his face when Janine turned dead white. "Oh, but I'm sure you wouldn't know anything about that."

Bo glanced from Sam to Janine and back again. His expression was blank as a mask, but the pain of Janine's betrayal—ancient history though it might be—shone in his eyes. "Janine? Is this true?"

She stumbled backward through the open door and into the foyer, her gaze glued to the floor. "Get out."

"No, Janine, wait, just—" Bo stopped, cursing, when the door slammed shut. Shaking off Sam's arm, he stalked forward and rapped on the door. "Janine. Come on, it doesn't matter anymore if you... It doesn't matter. It took both of us to destroy our marriage. Just please come back out and let's talk."

"No," she called through the door. "Now get the fuck off my porch or I'm calling the police."

Sam laid a tentative hand on Bo's shoulder. "Come on, Bo. Let's just leave."

Bo shook him off again. "I'm not leaving." He pounded the door with his fist. "Janine, goddammit. Don't do this."

Sam glanced behind him, half expecting to see a patrol car coming up the street. "Bo, let's go. We can deal with this later, when everyone's not so angry."

With a snarl that made Sam back up a pace, Bo whirled to face him. "I fucking *told* you to wait in the car. I *told* you you'd just set her off. So *fuck* you."

That stung. The fact that Bo was right just made it hurt worse. Sam wrapped his arms around himself. "I'm sorry."

"Save it." Pivoting around again, Bo banged both palms against the heavy wood. "Janine, you can't get away with this. I won't let you."

A sharp rap rattled the window a few feet away. Sam and Bo both turned to look. Janine stood in the window, the phone pressed to her ear. *Cops,* she mouthed, pointing at the phone.

Nervous, Sam glanced around. The couple next door were standing on their porch, watching. Out on the sidewalk, a young man walking his dog stopped to stare. *Shit.*

Sam stepped up to Bo and grabbed his arm. "We need to leave. Right now."

"No."

"Yes." Sam slid an arm around Bo's waist and tried to guide him away from the door. Bo shoved him away, and Sam fought not to let his frustration get the better of him. "People are watching us, Bo. The police are coming. Do you really want to stay here and possibly be arrested?"

Some of the fevered light went out of Bo's eyes. He looked toward the neighbors, then back to the front door barring him from his children.

For a second, Sam thought he was going to give in and leave without a fight. Then Adrian's panicked voice floated from behind the door. "Dad! I wanna come with you!"

"Adrian?" Bo grabbed the doorknob and twisted. It didn't budge. He kicked the door. "Janine, fuck! Let me see him!"

On the far end of the street, a police cruiser came into view. Adrian's muffled wail sounded, begging his mother to let him go with his dad.

Bo kicked the door again, then slammed both fists against it. "Fuck, open this *fucking door!*"

Sam glanced down the street. The patrol car was only a couple of blocks away.

They were out of time.

"Sorry about this, Bo." Wrapping both arms around Bo's waist, Sam dragged him backward across the porch.

Bo struggled wildly in Sam's grip. "Let me go, dammit."

"No," Sam panted, hauling Bo down the steps. "You'll thank me for this later."

"Fuck you." With a sudden, swift twist, Bo broke out of Sam's arms and lunged for the steps.

Grabbing Bo's shoulders, Sam spun him around to put them face to face. "Bo, if you want to see your kids again, we need to leave. Now."

Bo stilled in Sam's grip. His wide eyes searched Sam's face. After a second that seemed to last forever, he nodded.

Relieved, Sam led Bo to the car and pushed him into the passenger seat, then hurried to get behind the wheel and start the engine. He backed into the street just as the police cruiser passed the house at the end of the block.

Holding his breath, Sam shifted into drive and started up the street at a slow pace. If the cops were going to chase him, they'd catch him no matter how fast he sped off, and the last thing he wanted was to look like he was running. He and Bo hadn't actually done anything illegal, as far he knew. Maybe the officers would simply talk to Janine and let him and Bo go.

When no sirens sounded behind him, Sam glanced in the

rearview mirror. To his surprise, the police vehicle rolled right past Janine's house and turned left at the next corner. A regular patrol, Sam realized, and not a response to an emergency call.

That fucking sneaky bitch, she never called the cops. She faked us out. Sam snorted.

Bo shot him a glance full of barely contained anger. "What the hell are you laughing at?"

Sam shook his head. "Nothing. Just...reaction. Sorry."

He didn't mention the lack of police presence at Janine's house. The last thing Bo needed right now was an excuse to go back.

Bo settled against the seat, both hands fisted in his lap and his face turned away from Sam. He didn't say a word, but Sam felt his fury, his helplessness and his fear.

Sam drove home instead of going back to the office, reasoning that neither of them had any real work left to do. If Bo had any objection to that plan, he kept it to himself, which was fine with Sam. Andre would make sure Bo's work was saved and his computer shut down before leaving.

Part of Sam wished they could go back to the more neutral ground of the office, but he knew there was no point. Sooner or later, Bo was going to have some very ugly things to say to Sam. Those things might as well be said at home, in private.

God, I really fucked up. Is there any way he's going to forgive me?

The possibility that he wouldn't made Sam's stomach churn. He gritted his teeth against the bile rising in his throat.

The short trip passed in a silence so tense it made Sam's skin itch. By the time they entered their apartment, Sam felt ready to scream. He wished Bo would just say whatever he had to say and get it out there. Waiting for the cutting words Sam knew were coming was unbearable.

Bo shuffled over to the sofa and plopped into one corner. He curled forward, burying his face in his hands. "Fuck."

Sam's heart twisted. He walked over to the couch and sat beside Bo. Unsure of his welcome, he brushed hesitant fingers against Bo's arm. "I'm sorry, Bo."

Bo let out a brittle laugh, muffled by his hands. "Yeah. You're sorry *now,* when the damage is done." He lifted his head, aiming an icy glare at Sam. "You may have just cost me my kids, Sam. Why can't you just stay out of things that are none of your business?"

Believing Bo would blame him and knowing it were two very different things. Hearing it out loud felt like being sliced open. Sam folded his arms over his belly as if staunching a physical wound.

"I'm sorry," Sam repeated, knowing it wasn't good enough but not knowing what else he *could* say. "I'd go back and change things if I could."

"Yeah, well, you can't." Bo pushed to his feet and started pacing, one hand twisting the tail of his braid. "Fuck, Sam. *Fuck.* Why couldn't you just keep your fucking mouth shut for once?"

Anger stirred in Sam's chest in spite of himself. "Look, I know I screwed up. As you pointed out already, I can't change what happened. I'll just have to live with my mistake."

"You? *You're* going to have to live with it?" Bo stopped and stabbed a finger at Sam's chest. "*I'm* going to have to live with it, Sam. My kids are going to have to live with it. So *fuck* you."

Rising to his feet, Sam walked across the room and away from the temptation to hit Bo. "I doubt things would've gone any differently in the end, anyway. She wasn't going to listen to you. That much was obvious from the start."

Bo stalked over to Sam, radiating pure fury like a furnace. "She would've come around eventually. I know her, I know how she is. She would've listened to me in the end."

"That's wishful thinking, Bo."

"No it isn't. She *would have* changed her mind. You fucked it up."

And you're fooling yourself. Sam took a deep breath, trying to tamp down the anger he had no right to feel. It was like trying to stop the tide with a wall of twigs. "You weren't helping your own case, losing your cool like that."

"Losing my cool? My sons are in danger, and I can't save them from it, and you expect me to keep my cool?" Bo laughed, the sound edged with hysteria. "Shit. Oh, shit."

Stepping closer, Sam reached for Bo. He stumbled away from Sam's touch. "Bo, come on," Sam pleaded. "Just—"

"Shut *up.*" Bo's anguished gaze darted around the room. Snatching an empty glass off the windowsill, he threw it against the opposite wall. It shattered, littering the floor with bits of glass.

"Fuck!" Bo screamed. "Fuck, fuck, *fuck!*"

Frightened and aching in sympathy for Bo, Sam pulled him close and wrapped both arms securely around him. He held on when Bo struggled, refusing to let go even when Bo's fists started pummeling his back.

Sam yelped when Bo's teeth dug into his neck hard enough to draw blood. Grabbing Bo's braid, Sam yanked his head back. "Stop it, Bo. You're hurting me."

"Good. I want you to hurt." Bo got his arms between himself and Sam and pushed, breaking Sam's hold on him. Lifting a shaking hand, he wiped Sam's blood from his lips. He stared at the red stain on his fingers, then lifted his gaze to meet Sam's.

Sam stared back, his heart racing. Somewhere between one look and the next, the fire in Bo's eyes had gone from angry to lustful, and Sam's body reacted accordingly. He licked his dry lips, torn between fear and a sudden, fierce need.

Before he could decide what to do about the sexual energy crackling between them, Bo took the decision from him by fisting both hands in Sam's hair and kissing him.

There was nothing sweet or tender about this kiss. It was brutal, invasive, full of rage. Sam felt his lips bruise under the assault, felt Bo's fingers skating down his spine to dig painfully into his lower back, and God, it was perfect. Sam clutched Bo close and let himself be ravaged.

Pulling back, Bo planted both hands on Sam's chest and shoved. Sam went tumbling backward onto the floor, landing on his hip. A sharp pain shot up his side. Dazed, he didn't fight when Bo rolled him onto his back and started undoing his jeans.

A low moan tore from Sam's chest when Bo yanked off his shoes, pants and underwear, tossed them aside and bent to suck hard on the head of his cock. "Bo. God."

Letting go of Sam's erection, Bo stood, toed off his shoes and shed his jeans and boxer-briefs. He tore off his shirt, then sank down to straddle Sam's thighs. "Get the lube."

For a moment, Sam had no idea what Bo meant. Then he remembered the tube of K-Y Bo had hidden under the chair a few weeks ago. *For emergencies,* he'd said, after the second time in as many days that they'd gotten carried away in the living room and had to interrupt themselves to return to the bedroom for lube.

Stretching backward, Sam reached beneath the chair and

felt around for the little tube. He found it, drew it out and handed it to Bo.

Sam expected Bo to get up, spread Sam's legs and push inside him. Instead, Bo squeezed gel into his palm and coated Sam's prick with it.

"Oh God," Sam breathed. The feel of Bo's hands on his cock was almost enough to make him come right then. "Stop. Stop. Gonna come if you...if you keep doing that."

Bo let go, sat up on his knees and scooted forward. He grabbed Sam's slick cock, pressed the head against his hole and drove his hips downward, impaling himself on Sam's shaft.

Sam gasped, his body arching off the floor. Above him, Bo shuddered, his face contorting with a mix of pleasure and pain. Sam grasped Bo's hipbones in both hands and fought to stay still. The undulating grip of Bo's insides felt so good it scared him. If he lost control and started thrusting too soon, he could damage Bo, and he'd never forgive himself if that happened. Especially now, with both of their emotions flayed raw.

"Move," Bo whispered, so low Sam barely heard him.

Sam stared up into Bo's half-lidded eyes, trying to read the expression there through the lustful fog in his brain. "Bo, I don't—"

"Move." Bo's pelvis swung forward and back, forward and back, drawing an agonized whimper from Sam's throat. "Fuck me."

"But—"

Bo's eyelids flew up, his gaze burning into Sam's. "Please. I need it."

Sam wanted to protest. But Bo rose up and slammed himself down again, making them both cry out, and Sam couldn't hold out any longer. Bending his knees, he braced his heels on the floor and drove his cock up into Bo.

Falling forward, Bo planted his hands on Sam's chest. His braid swung over his shoulder to brush Sam's skin. "Yes. God. Harder."

Sam groaned, unable to speak. The entire universe seemed centered on his prick, on the hot grip of Bo's ass around him, so good it hurt. He snapped his groin upward so hard he nearly knocked Bo off of him.

Bo's thighs tightened around Sam's hips, his fingers digging deep into Sam's pectorals. Sam's next thrust sent a drop of pre-come tumbling from the tip of Bo's cock to splash onto Sam's belly. Moved by a sudden urge to taste, Sam swiped the clear fluid onto his finger and sucked it off.

"Oh God," Bo moaned, his cheeks flushing red as he watched Sam's tongue. "Please..."

Sam's fist was already closing around Bo's shaft before he consciously realized it. After more than a year together, knowing when and how Bo wanted to be touched was almost a reflex. Bo's knowledge of Sam's body was just as deep. The thought of losing that intimacy forever made Sam's throat close up and his eyes sting.

Bo's hips seesawed. The friction sent electric jolts from Sam's prick directly to his brain, blasting away the fear of Bo leaving him. Bo loved him. Loved him in spite of his flaws, in spite of how often or how badly he fucked up, and Sam felt the same about him. Together, they had the strength to survive the current disaster.

Whether or not Bo would survive as a father wasn't so clear.

Don't think of that. Not now.

Sam tightened his grip on Bo's cock, pulling hard and fast. "Come," he panted, staring up into Bo's eyes. "Come on."

A soft keening escaped Bo's lips. His cock pulsed and spurted in Sam's hand, his semen spattering Sam's chest and belly. A warm, sticky drop landed on Sam's lip. He licked it off.

Bo's hole clamped down hard on Sam's prick, and the feeling was too intense to fight. Not that Sam wanted to. He moaned Bo's name as his orgasm rolled over him.

Bo collapsed forward onto Sam's chest. They both hissed as the movement dislodged Sam's cock. Sam's entire body felt weak and heavy, but he brought his arms up to hold Bo close. Closing his eyes, he buried his face in Bo's hair and breathed in the scents of shampoo, skin and sex.

After a moment, Bo's shoulders began to shake and Sam felt a telltale dampness against his neck. He stroked Bo's bare back, kissed his hair, whispered words of love and impossible promises into his ear. Sam barely noticed his own tears.

It took a while for Bo's silent grief to ease. When he finally lay still and quiet in Sam's arms, Sam let exhaustion and post-coital lethargy pull him down into welcome oblivion.

∞

Sam, miraculously and horribly fifteen again, cowered in a corner of the high school basement. Above him stomped an unseen menace, rattling the ceiling and sending spiders scurrying into cracks in the walls. Sam curled up tighter. If he stayed here, the monster wouldn't find him.

A shrill noise split the air. The bell ringing, calling students to class. Calling Sam from his hiding place to face what had to be faced.

"No!" he screamed. "I don't want to! Don't make me!"

"You can't hide forever," boomed the monster from the floor

above. "You have to answer it. Here I come..."

Sam bolted upright with a shout. Panting, he darted a wide-eyed gaze around the room. Bo, standing naked beside the sofa, glanced at Sam before reaching for the phone...

The phone. It was the phone ringing.

Sam hauled himself to his feet as the lingering traces of the nightmare dissipated. His lips curved into a wry smile. A psychologist would have a field day with *that* dream.

"What? Wait, Sean, just calm down and—" Bo stopped, cut off by the high, panicked voice of his son.

Sam frowned. He couldn't make out what Sean was saying, but he sounded terrified. What the hell was going on?

Bo caught his eye. Sam raised his eyebrows in silent inquiry, and Bo shook his head. "Sean. Son, I can't understand you. Take a deep breath, calm down and say it again, okay?"

Sam leaned closer. This time, Sean's words came through loud and clear. "Dad, Adrian's making the monsters come!"

Chapter Thirteen

Bo's face went gray. "Sean, God. Get out, okay? All of you, get out of the house if you can and just *run*. We're on our way."

Through the mouthpiece of the phone, Sam heard Adrian's sobs. "The doors won't open. Hurry, Dad, we—"

The line went dead.

Sam and Bo stared at each other for a second. Then Bo dropped the phone and jumped to his feet. Sam followed.

Within two minutes, they were dressed and running out the door. Sam had no idea what time it was, but darkness had fallen and a cold drizzle had begun. He snatched the car keys from Bo's hand. "I'm driving."

Bo didn't argue, just slid into the passenger seat. His hands clutched at the dashboard as Sam squealed out of their parking spot and out into the street.

Sam drove as fast as he dared on the wet road, keeping his eyes peeled for police. Being stopped for speeding might prove fatal to the terrified people trapped in Janine and Lee's house.

"When we get there, I'll start working on closing the portal while you find the kids," Sam said, taking the turn into Janine's neighborhood on two wheels.

"How do we get in? Sean said the door wouldn't...wouldn't open."

The way Bo's voice broke made Sam's heart ache, but he ignored it. There wasn't time for emotion right now. "Hopefully we can force it open. If not, we'll break a window and go in that way."

Bo nodded. "I wish I knew where in the house they are. I—" Bo's eyes went wide, a horrified gasp escaping his lips as Janine's house came into view ahead. "Sam, oh my God."

Sam looked, and his stomach knotted with cold dread. A grayish fog shrouded the house, smoky tendrils creeping across the yard and reaching toward the sky. The house bent and wavered, distorted by the strange miasma.

"Shit." Pushing the accelerator to the floor, Sam sped halfway over the curb and onto the lawn of the house. He cut the engine, jumped out of the car and ran toward the house as fast as he could, with Bo at his heels.

The fog was freezing cold, turning his breath to white mist. The frozen grass crunched beneath his feet. Taking the steps two at a time, he grabbed the doorknob. He felt the metal freeze to his palm. "Sean!" he shouted. "Adrian! We're here, we're trying to get in."

A faint wail, high and desperate, floated from somewhere upstairs. To Sam's left, Bo hefted one of the wrought-iron chairs sitting on the porch and threw it through the bay window. Glass exploded everywhere. Bo plunged through the opening.

Cursing, Sam tore his hand from the doorknob, leaving a strip of bloody skin behind. He leaped through the broken window, ignoring the sting of glass slicing his arms and face. "Bo! Where are you?"

Bo's voice called back to him, faint and muffled, but Sam couldn't tell where it was coming from. He looked around. The walls curved in ways they shouldn't, the hallway twisting into blackness. Sam felt as if he were standing in a carnival funhouse.

Panic seized him. He stood frozen with indecision. Where was Bo? Where were the boys? Were they even still alive?

What the fuck do I do now?

A deep, wordless sound rasped through the air. In its wake came a childish scream.

Sean.

The sound broke Sam's paralysis. Opening his mind, he braced himself for the onslaught of malicious intent from beyond the dimensional barrier. When it hit, he nearly buckled under it. Gasping for breath, he forced himself to his feet and followed the thread of searing energy up the stairs.

The creature crouched in the middle of the upstairs hall, a hulking mass of shadow. Watching it was like staring at a black light. Its form blurred, moved and shifted.

Except for the claws. The serrated claws, black and gleaming in the weak illumination of the hall light.

"Sean!" Sam called. "Where are you?"

To Sam's relief, Janine's voice cut through Sean's renewed cries. "Here. God, help me, I c-can't stop it."

Keeping his mind focused on the horror in front of him, Sam bounded up the last few stairs and stopped a few feet short of the creature. This close, the cold was enough to numb Sam's fingers. His heart jumped into his throat when he saw Sean curled in the corner, whimpering pitifully.

Janine stood between her son and the creature, white-faced and plainly terrified, a kitchen knife clutched in one shaking hand. Her panic-glazed eyes cut toward Sam. "S-Sean. Sean."

Sam knew what she was trying to say. *Save Sean. Don't let it hurt him.*

Sam wanted to answer, to tell her that he'd die before he let that thing hurt anyone else. But he felt the thing's attention shift, felt its awareness of him, and knew there wasn't a second to spare. It knew who he was, and what he could do. Its malice thumped through his blood. He had to act, before it butchered Sean and Janine for no other reason than just because it could.

Closing his eyes, Sam found the umbilical cord linking the creature to its own reality and focused every ounce of his concentration on it. He felt the thing's resistance, felt the bloodlust that drove it. Its presence spread like a dark stain through Sam's consciousness, driving him to hands and knees in the hallway, and he realized in a burst of unwelcome insight that he wasn't strong enough to send it back. The portal—*portals*, he understood suddenly, feeling the multiple open gateways in his mind—were too powerful.

His eyes flew open. He was about to fail. Again. Despair washed over him.

Maybe you can't beat it, but you can hold it back for a little while. Long enough for them to get away.

"Run," he gasped. "Find Bo and Adrian, and Lee, and get out. I can't hold it long."

Through his darkening vision, he thought he saw Janine scoop Sean into her arms and leap past the creature. She shouted something, but he couldn't hear her past the static in his head, and couldn't have answered anyway. His lungs were on fire, his heart laboring to pump his blood. He wasn't going to last long before he passed out. Why wasn't Janine running like he'd told her to? Why wasn't she getting her sons out of there?

With startling abruptness, the pressure squeezing Sam's chest eased, and he could breathe again. He raised his head and was shocked to see Adrian standing at the top of the stairs, his face screwed up in concentration, brown eyes fixed on the monster not five feet from him. The thing began to fade, its form losing solidity.

Adrian was trying to send it back and close the portal. And it was working.

A surge of hope sent Sam stumbling to his feet. Standing beside Adrian, he focused his mind once more on the open portal. He pushed, felt Adrian's energy pushing as well. The creature hissed and scuttled toward them, claws clicking on the wood. Sam stepped in front of Adrian, redoubling his efforts. Somewhere behind him, Sean screamed over and over and over again.

Sam opened his mouth to tell Adrian to run, he felt the thing's resistance give way, and in an instant it was gone. Sam sent psychic feelers through the house, searching for any signs of the portals he'd felt before, or of the things that inhabited the other side.

There was nothing. Just the flat metallic taste of permanently closed gateways.

Sam's knees gave out, and he slumped to the floor. Adrian plopped down beside him, his face blank.

"Adrian?" Sam reached out to touch the boy's shoulder. "Are you okay?"

"Are they gone?" Adrian whispered, the quaver in his voice the only indication of his fear. "Is it over?"

"Yes, it's over. We did it. The portals are closed, and those things are gone."

Adrian turned to look at him, dark eyes haunted. "Where's Dad?"

"Right here."

Sam twisted around, and nearly fainted with relief at seeing Bo alive and unhurt, running up the stairs. Bo fell to his knees and gathered Adrian into his arms. "Adrian. God. I couldn't get to you. I heard you, but I couldn't...couldn't find the stairs. Shit."

Adrian's arms went around Bo's neck, slowly, as if he couldn't believe Bo was really there. "Dad?"

"Yes." Bo let out a sobbing laugh. "It's okay, son. It's okay. I've got you."

Adrian blinked a couple of times, then his face crumpled. He clung to Bo and sobbed, his small body shaking in Bo's arms. Bo sat on the floor and rocked him, whispering soothing words into his hair.

Sam crawled closer and sat beside Bo, one arm around Bo's shoulders. Looking around, he noticed Lee for the first time, sitting with his back against the far wall of the hallway. Janine leaned into the curve of his arm, with Sean huddled on her lap.

"Y'all okay?" Sam asked. His voice sounded hoarse and rough.

Lee nodded. "I think so. Physically, anyway." He laid a hand on the back of Sean's head, his expression solemn. Sean whimpered and pressed tighter against his mother.

Janine rested her cheek on the boy's head and rubbed soothing circles on his back. Her gaze caught Sam's and held it. "Thank you."

Sam smiled. "Any time."

Janine smiled back, and Sam thought maybe there was hope for them after all.

∞

Tearing off a strip of silk tape, Dean secured the gauze

wrap to Sam's hand. "There. That should protect it well enough. Make sure you keep it clean, keep the antibiotic ointment on it, and change the bandage twice a day." He shook his head, lips pursing. "You'll have to keep an eye on all these glass cuts too. They're mostly little, they should heal fine, but still. Keep 'em clean."

"Got it." Sam flexed his hand, wincing. Now that the excitement was over and the adrenaline rush had drained away, his hand throbbed with pain where the piece of skin had been torn from his palm on the frozen doorknob. "Ow."

"Let me get your neck fixed up, then I'll be done. You can take some Ibuprofen for the pain when you get home." Dean dug through the first-aid kit on the dining room table, emerging with a large Band-Aid. He set it on the table beside the gauze squares, peroxide and antibiotic ointment. "You really should've called EMS instead of calling me, you know. Turn your head to the right a little."

Sam obediently turned his head so Dean could clean and bandage the broken skin where Bo had bitten him earlier. "For cuts and scrapes? Naw, no need. Besides, they would've asked a lot of awkward questions."

"Yeah, there's that. Although it might've been a good idea to have the kids checked out, just in case."

"You looked them over and said they seemed to be okay."

"They did, but I'm not a doctor, just a nurse's aid with ER experience. But I totally understand, so I won't fuss at you too hard." Dean stuck the Band-Aid on Sam's neck and patted his shoulder. "There you go. Good as new."

"Thanks."

"No problem." Dean shot him a wry grin. "Not like I had anything else to do."

"Don't you have plans for Thanksgiving?"

"Not really. Thought I'd just veg out at home. Watch some movies or something, you know?"

It sounded like a lonely holiday to Sam, but he knew better than to say so, or to ask Dean why he wasn't spending the day with his family. Dean always managed to steer the conversation away from himself.

Lee walked in, a duffle bag in each hand. "Here are the boys' things. Enough for tonight, anyway. We'll regroup tomorrow."

Sam nodded. "Sounds good. It was good of you and Janine to let the kids stay with us tonight."

"We agreed it would be better for them to be with you and Bo in a familiar environment than to stay with Janine and me in a motel. We're glad the two of you were able to take the boys for a while. The window's easily fixed, but I can't imagine either of the kids would feel comfortable here any longer."

"So what are y'all gonna do?" Dean asked as he put away the first-aid supplies. "Are you gonna look for a new place?"

"I suppose so." Lee scanned the room, his expression sad. "It's a shame. Janine and I did love this house. But we can't stay here. None of us would ever sleep again, I'm sure."

"Well, the portals are permanently closed, so it should be safe to sell, at least." Sam looked past Lee to the empty foyer. "Is Bo still upstairs?"

"Yes. He's talking with Sean."

"How's he doing?" Bag in hand, Dean walked over to stand beside Sam and Lee. "Him and Adrian both. This must've been pretty horrible for them."

"It was." Lee sighed. "Sean's calmed down, but he's scared to death to be by himself right now. Adrian? I don't know. He *seems* okay. But you know how he is, Sam. He keeps things to himself. I think I'm more worried about him than Sean."

"Yeah, me too." Sam ran a thumb over the gauze wrapped around his hand. "I know Bo's talked to him, but I think I should too sometime in the next couple of days. I know what he's feeling right now. I think I can help."

"Yes, I believe you can." Lee gave him a tired smile. "We all owe you our lives, Sam. I don't know how to thank you."

Footsteps sounded on the stairs. Sam looked up in time to see Janine walk in, with Adrian beside her. Heat flooded Sam's face. "You should thank Adrian. He's the one who closed those portals. I wasn't strong enough."

"You taught me." Adrian regarded Sam with solemn eyes, red-rimmed from crying. "I wouldn't have known how to focus if you hadn't. And I could feel your mind there, helping me. I couldn't have made those things go away by myself."

Janine walked forward, both arms wrapped around herself as if to hold herself together. She stared up into Sam's face. "My kids nearly died tonight because of me. Because I didn't believe you and Bo, or Adrian. Because I didn't listen. I wish I had. I'm sorry."

Sam shrugged, feeling horribly awkward. "You were doing what you thought was best. I'll be the first to admit that all the portal stuff seems pretty out there until you've seen it for yourself."

"It does, yes. But it's real." She looked down at the floor, then back up at Sam, her eyes full of remorse. "I've been awful to you and Bo both. I'm not even sure why, just..." She drew a deep breath and blew it out. "I know there's a lot of bad blood between us. But I'd like to start over, if you're willing to forgive me."

Sam smiled. "Only if you're willing to forgive me for all the ugly things I've said."

She let out a nervous laugh. "Deal."

Sam held out his uninjured hand. "Shake."

She clasped his hand, and they shook. At that moment Bo entered the room with Sean in his arms. His eyebrows went up. "What's going on?"

Janine turned to smile at him. "Sam and I have agreed to bury the hatchet."

Bo beamed at them both. "That's wonderful. Thank you both for being willing to set aside your differences."

Letting go of Sam's hand, Janine walked over and kissed Sean's head. "I'm burying the hatchet with you too, Bo. I'll call my lawyer Friday. I still think we should work out a new custody agreement, but I've decided that it should include equal time with the boys for both of us. I'd also like for all of us—you, Sam, Lee and myself—to spend more time together. I think it would give the boys a more stable environment."

Provided we can all get along. Sam kept the small doubt private. He knew from personal experience that nothing changed your perspective quite like almost dying. If tonight's experience couldn't change their group dynamic for the better, nothing could.

The smile on Bo's face lit up the room. "I agree."

Dean cleared his throat. "Okay, I'm off. Y'all take care."

He waved and walked through the foyer to the door, followed by a chorus of goodbyes. Sam walked beside him out onto the porch. "Thanks for coming over, Dean. Maybe it's dumb, but I'd really rather have you patch me up than some paramedic."

Dean laughed. "Well, dumb or not, I don't mind doing it. Just make sure you call me if it gets worse. I'll look at it and tell you if you need to see a doctor."

"I will." Gazing around the dark, quiet neighborhood, Sam shook his head. "I still can't believe none of the neighbors called the cops."

"Maybe they did. Maybe the 911 operator didn't believe them."

"Oh my God, would they really say they don't believe someone?"

"Hm, let's think this through." Dean held his thumb and pinkie up to his head, mimicking a phone. "Hello, 911? Yes, my neighbor's house is shrouded in otherwordly fog and is about to fall into another dimension. There might be monsters too." His eyes widened in mock surprise. "No, I haven't been drinking, why do you ask?"

Sam laughed. "Okay, I see your point."

"Uh-huh. Just be glad either no one noticed or they couldn't get anyone to come out, because the cops would *not* have been amused by your story."

"Tell me about it." Sam reached out to touch Dean's shoulder. "Hey, you want to come over tomorrow?"

Dean blinked, obviously shocked by the invitation. "Tomorrow's Thanksgiving."

"I know. That's why I'm inviting you."

"But you and Bo have the kids, and—"

"And Bo's going to invite Lee and Janine over for Thanksgiving dinner, since they can't be here at their house, and there's always room for a friend." Sam shrugged. "I don't like to think of you being alone."

Dean stared at him for a moment, then pulled him into a tight hug. "Thanks, Sam."

"Hey, it'll be great to have you there." With a pat on Dean's back, Sam pulled away. "We're not eating until around six, since we're going to have to make a trip to the store first, but you can come over any time."

"All right. See you tomorrow, then." Grinning, Dean descended the steps and climbed into his green Civic. Bo, Lee, Janine and the boys walked out onto the porch as Dean backed into the street. He waved before driving away.

Sam slid an arm around Bo's waist. "Dean's coming over for Thanksgiving dinner tomorrow. I hope that's okay."

"Of course it is. He never seems to spend time with his family on holidays, and it worries me how often he's alone." Bo shifted his grip on Sean, who had fallen into an exhausted sleep on his father's shoulder. "Janine, I wish you and Lee would stay with us. The sofa makes out into a bed, Sam and I would be glad to camp out there for a while."

Janine shook her head. "We don't want to intrude. And I know we would be, no matter what you say." She slipped her hand through Lee's elbow and leaned against his arm. "Lee's sister gets back in town Sunday. We can stay with her while we're looking for a new place. She has plenty of room. In the meantime, we can afford a motel room for a few days."

"Thank you for inviting us for Thanksgiving," Lee added.

"We're happy to have you." Bo turned to look at Sam. "You ready to go?"

"More than ready." Twisting around, Sam smiled at Adrian, who stood silent and uncharacteristically pale beside his mother. "Adrian, can you open the car door for your dad? He's kind of got his hands full. I'll get yours and Sean's bags."

"'Kay." Adrian slipped both arms around Janine's waist and squeezed. "I love you, Mom."

Tears welled in Janine's eyes. She bent and hugged Adrian hard. "I love you too, sweetheart. We'll see you tomorrow."

Nodding, Adrian pulled away. He hesitated only a moment before giving Lee a brief hug as well. "'Night, Lee."

Lee patted Adrian's back. "Good night. See you tomorrow."

Sam followed Bo and the boys out to the car and got behind the wheel while Bo settled Sean into the backseat. He set the bags beside the car and popped the trunk so Bo could stow them.

Adrian plopped into the seat beside his still-sleeping brother. Sam watched him in the rearview mirror. "You did good tonight, Adrian."

Adrian's lip trembled. "I was scared, and Mom got mad because I wanted to live with Dad, and that made *me* mad and..." The boy hung his head so that Sam could no longer see his face. "I let them out. It was my fault."

The whispered words overflowed with guilt and fear, and Sam felt a stab of empathy. He knew what guilt felt like. How it could weigh a person down.

"It wasn't your fault," he said. "Those things, whatever they are and wherever they come from, they know how to use our emotions against us. They find people like us, who have these special abilities, and they use us to get to our world." Struck by a sudden idea, he twisted around to study Adrian across the back of the seat. "Did you feel like you could hear them, in your head? Like they were talking to you, only without words?"

Adrian's head snapped up, his eyes huge. "Yeah. I thought..."

He trailed off, but Sam thought he knew what the boy was thinking. The same thing he himself had wondered at Oleander House, when the dreams plagued him and the alien thoughts invaded his mind night and day. *I thought I was going crazy.*

"You're not crazy," Sam told him just as Bo climbed into the front seat. "I hear them too."

Bo darted an apprehensive look between the two of them. "Hear what?"

Turning back around, Sam gave Bo's hand a quick squeeze before starting the car. "We were just talking about the portals. It helps to talk about it."

Bo nodded. He glanced over his shoulder at Adrian. "Are you okay, son?"

"Yeah." Adrian leaned against the seat and stared out the window. "Just tired."

"I know you must be. Go on to sleep, if you want." Bo gave his son a sympathetic smile before turning to face front again.

They made the drive home in silence. By the time they reached their apartment and got the boys inside, Adrian's eyelids were drooping. He brushed his teeth and changed into his pajamas and was sound asleep by the time his head hit the pillow. Sean slept right through being carried upstairs and tucked into bed. Bo kissed both boys' heads before switching off the light and following Sam into their own room.

"What does Adrian hear that you're hearing too?" Bo finally asked after he and Sam had gotten ready for bed and lay curled together beneath the covers. "And why did he think he was crazy? He already knew the portals were real."

"The beings on the other side can communicate with him. They talk to him, just like they do to me."

Bo made a small, distressed noise. "Oh my God, Sam. What do we do? How do we stop it?"

Sam could barely see Bo's face in the dark room, but he knew the man must be horrified by what he'd just said.

"We don't." Sam touched a finger to Bo's lips to stop his outraged protest. "I've been thinking about this all the way home, and I think that level of connection might be why Adrian and I can act as a conduit without becoming catatonic. I think that might also be why those things don't seem to harm us."

Bo's eyes glittered in the dimness, searching Sam's face. "Are you sure?"

"No. I don't think there's any way to be completely sure. But it makes sense to me. He not only got through tonight without being harmed, mentally or physically, he also managed to shut down multiple developing portals with minimal help from me." Sliding one hand around the back of Bo's neck, Sam pulled him close and kissed his forehead. "Judging by what I felt tonight, Adrian's psychokinetic powers are much stronger than mine. There's no telling what he might be able to do with the right kind of direction."

Bo was silent for a while, one hand caressing Sam's hip. "You've helped him a great deal so far. Can you help him learn to deal with...what he can do?"

"I'll do my best. But honestly, I think he needs more help than I can give him."

Bo scooted closer and rested his forehead against Sam's. "What can we do to help him?"

"I'm not sure," Sam admitted. "But I'll find out."

Sam saw Bo's smile even in the dark. Hands tangling in Sam's hair, Bo pulled him close and kissed him. Their tongues wound together, and the feel of it set a fire in Sam's belly, just as it always did.

"I love you," Bo whispered against Sam's lips.

"I love you." Tilting his head, Sam nuzzled Bo's cheek. "Go to sleep. You're worn out."

With a soft sigh, Bo settled against Sam's chest, his head tucked under Sam's chin and one arm around Sam's waist. He was asleep in minutes, his slow, even breaths tickling Sam's throat.

Sam lay awake, stroking Bo's back and thinking. Undoubtedly, the weeks and months ahead would be hard on multiple levels. Adrian still had to come to terms with a talent which set him apart. Sam, Bo, Janine and Lee all had their work cut out for them in learning to get along, and to see each other in a new light. Tonight, however, marked a major turning point in all their lives, and it gave Sam real hope for their collective future.

Shutting his eyes, Sam concentrated on the scent of Bo's hair, the sound of his breathing, the solid warmth of his body. Within moments, Sam drifted into a deep, untroubled sleep, with Bo's heart beating slow and steady against his chest.

Epilogue

It was warm for December. Fifty-two degrees, even though the sun had almost set below the moss-hung oaks to the west.

Sam leaned his elbows against the rail of the deck and gazed out over the stretch of thin winter grass to Mobile Bay, lapping at the sand about fifty feet from the back of Lee and Janine's new house. The waning sunset tipped the choppy waves with faint gold. Across the bay, lights clustered on the dark hump of the Eastern Shore.

The whole thing made for a peaceful Christmas picture. Sam smiled, breathing in the clean salt scent.

Behind him, he heard the French double doors open and close. Footsteps clumped across the deck. Arms wound around his waist, and a hard body pressed to his back. He leaned into the embrace, tilting his head for the warm lips kissing his neck. "Hi, Bo."

"Hi." Bo nipped his earlobe. "Dinner's almost ready, are you coming in?"

"Mm-hm. Just checking out the view."

Bo's laugh rumbled against Sam's back. "You've checked out the view at least a dozen times since we arrived this morning. Anyone would think this is the first time you've been here."

"Yeah, well, we were always too busy before to spend much time out here. Besides, the view at midafternoon is not the same as the view at sunset."

"True." Tightening his arms around Sam, Bo rested his chin on Sam's shoulder. "It really is beautiful here. I can't believe Lee and Janine found this house so quickly."

The couple had heard about the place from a realtor friend barely a week after the events at their old house. It needed work, but the price was in their range, and it was available immediately. They'd moved in a few days later, giving them just enough time to get halfway settled in before Christmas.

Sam still laughed every time he remembered the look on the realtor's face when the whole BCPI team showed up to check the new house before Janine and Lee would make an offer. He got the distinct feeling that most buyers did not require proof that a house was paranormally inactive before they would purchase it.

"I guess luck was on their side." Turning in Bo's arms, Sam cupped Bo's face in both hands. "God, you look amazing today."

"So you keep telling me."

"Only because it's true."

"Thank you. I could say the same to you, by the way." Bo grabbed Sam's ass and squeezed, grinning. "Kiss me, beautiful."

Sam happily complied. The kiss started out light and gentle, a bare brush of lips. It deepened and grew heated as Bo's mouth opened beneath Sam's, tongue pushing in. With a low groan, Sam dropped one hand from Bo's cheek and slipped it beneath the back of his sweater. The thin weave of the material clung to Bo's body, and the dark red color set off his hair and skin to perfection. Sam had been fighting the urge to jump him all day.

The sound of a throat clearing made them spring apart.

Sam glanced over Bo's shoulder to see Lee standing in the doorway, looking at once amused and uncomfortable. "Dinner's about ready."

With a swift, apologetic look at Sam, Bo turned around. "Thanks, Lee. We'll be in in a minute. We were just admiring the beautiful view."

Lee arched an eyebrow at them. "Yes, I can see that. Well, come on in when you get finished 'admiring the view'. Janine's making the gravy right now, and when that's done everything'll be ready."

Bo's blush was obvious, even in the waning light. "We're coming in now."

Taking Sam's hand in his, Bo led him through the French doors in Lee's wake. The door led directly into the combination kitchen and dining room. Dishes laden with traditional Christmas fare covered the long oval table, leaving barely a glimpse of the red and green tablecloth. The scents of turkey, sweet potato pie and Bo's homemade yeast rolls made Sam's mouth water.

"Mm. Smells good." Sam smiled at Janine, who stood at the stove pouring the gravy into a bowl. "I know I've already said this, but thank you both for having us over."

"It's our pleasure." Picking up the bowl, Janine carried it to the table. "It's the least we could do after you helped us get this place in shape in time for Christmas."

"There's still some work to be done." Letting go of Sam's hand, Bo hurried to the counter separating the kitchen area from the dining table and picked up the crystal bowl containing the cranberry sauce Danny had made for everyone at the office. "The deck needs re-staining before summer, and the front steps still need to be replaced."

"Yes, but the bulk of the outdoor work and all of the indoor is done, thanks to you and Sam." Janine surveyed the laden table. "I guess that's everything. Lee, would you call the boys, please?"

"Sure." Walking to the door, Lee leaned into the living room, where Sean and Adrian were playing. "Boys, dinner's ready."

Sam heard a loud whoop from Sean. Seconds later, the children came running into the dining room. Both boys were still laughing at whatever game they'd been playing.

It made Sam happy to see Adrian's wide smile and sparkling eyes. The two of them had met with a parapsychologist at the local college soon after Thanksgiving, and it had done the child a world of good. The woman had given Adrian plenty of practical tips on controlling and channeling his psychokinesis. She'd shown Sam how to help Adrian, and in the process helped Sam learn to better use his own talents. The end result had been increased confidence for them both, and that small change had worked wonders for Adrian.

Adrian plopped into the nearest chair. "Man, I'm starving."

"Me too." Lips pursed and hands on his hips, Sean studied the chairs gathered around the table. "Mom, can I sit next to Sam?"

Janine laughed. "You can sit wherever you like, honey."

"Cool." Bounding over to Sam, Sean grabbed his wrist and dragged him to one of the chairs on the opposite side of the table. "You sit here, Sam. Dad can sit on your other side."

"All right." Chuckling, Sam slid into the seat to which Sean pointed him. "Come on over, Bo."

Bo edged past Sean, heading for the chair on Sam's left. He stopped behind Sam, tilted his chin back and planted an upside down kiss on his lips before settling into the indicated chair.

His hand found Sam's knee under the table. Smiling, Sam curled his fingers around Bo's and squeezed.

If anyone had told him six months ago that he'd be spending Christmas Day with Bo's ex and her boyfriend along with the kids—and that they'd all be enjoying themselves—he'd have called that person crazy. Yet here they all were, sitting down to Christmas dinner together like a real family.

Things weren't perfect. Janine and Bo still fought sometimes, and she and Sam still irritated each other, but they were trying, and doing quite well for the most part. The new atmosphere of cooperation had been good for all of them, particularly the boys. Adrian smiled far more often than he scowled these days, and Sean's tendency toward hyperactivity had evened out.

If only they could banish the lingering reminders of that night in November. Sean was still terrified of being alone, and both children still suffered nightmares. At least Adrian had gained an impressive amount of control over his abilities, thanks to a lot of hard work and a level of determination Sam had never seen before in an adult, let alone an eleven-year-old.

A small hand tapping his shoulder brought Sam out of his thoughts. He glanced around, surprised to see everyone piling food onto their plates. He blinked at Sean. "Sorry, Sean, what did you say?"

"I said, would you please hand me a roll?"

"Sure." Reluctantly letting go of Bo's hand, Sam picked up the basket of rolls and passed it to Sean. "Here you go."

"Thanks." Sean snatched two and set them on top of his pile of turkey and dressing. "Dad makes *really* good rolls."

Sam laughed. "Yes, he does."

Bo nudged him with his shoulder. "Pass the green bean casserole, please."

For the next few minutes, Sam was kept busy filling his plate and passing bowls and platters around the table. The sounds of animated conversation and utensils clanking against plates nearly drowned out the soft Christmas music playing on the stereo in the living room.

Sam's Christmases growing up had never been like this—noisy, lively, messy. He loved it. If he got his way, the stiff, stifling Christmases of his youth would become a distant memory, replaced with more holidays like this one.

"Hey, Adrian." Sam smiled at the boy sitting across the table from him. "Would you pass me the salt, please?"

Picking up the salt shaker, Adrian held it across the table. Sam reached for it. His fingers were still a couple of inches away when the snowman-shaped container left Adrian's hand and floated into Sam's.

Floated. Without either of them touching it.

Oh, my God.

Eyes wide, Sam stared at Adrian. "Um. Thanks."

"Sure."

Adrian grinned, dark eyes twinkling, and Sam couldn't help grinning back.

It looked like life was about to get interesting.

Like things haven't been "interesting" enough the past year, he mused, sprinkling salt on his mashed potatoes.

One thing was certain. Life with Bo and his kids would never be boring. Sam snickered.

"What are you laughing at?" Bo asked, giving Sam's thigh a squeeze under the table.

"Huh? Oh, nothing." Sam met Bo's narrow-eyed glance with a bright smile. "Would you hand me the gravy?"

Reaching to his right, Bo picked up the gravy bowl and set

it in front of Sam's plate. Sam spooned gravy onto his potatoes, pretending not to see the curious looks Bo kept giving him. He could tell Bo about this latest development when they were alone. Right now, he wanted to relax and enjoy the festive family atmosphere.

The way he figured it, he'd earned this moment of peace. They all had.

With a wink at Adrian, Sam picked up his fork and dug in.

About the Author

Ally Blue is acknowledged by the world at large (or at least by her heroes, who tend to suffer a lot) as the Popess of Gay Angst. She has a great big penis hat and rides in a bullet-proof Plexiglas bubble in Christmas parades. Her harem of manwhores does double duty as bodyguards and as sinspirational entertainment. Her favorite band is Radiohead, her favorite color is lime green and her favorite way to waste a perfectly good Saturday is to watch all three extended version LOTR movies in a row. Her ultimate dream is to one day ditch the evil day job and support the family on manlove alone. She is not a hippie or a brain surgeon, no matter what her kids' friends say.

Marked as prey, Alec refuses to fall for a werewolf.
Until he's forced to turn to Liam for protection.

Marked
© *2007 Joely Skye*

Alec Ryerson carries a scar over his heart and scars on his psyche, ugly reminders of a nightmare that still doesn't seem quite real. Even a year later, he stays inside on full-moon nights and avoids most people—until he meets the strange and beautiful Liam.

Liam feels an undeniable pull toward Alec. However Liam is a werewolf; Alec is a human who clearly has trepidations about a relationship. Then Liam discovers he is not the first werewolf Alec has encountered. Alec has been marked for death by the murderous "quad", a group of twisted werewolves who prey on humans. Now the quad's sights are set on recruiting Liam's eight-year-old brother into their murderous pack.

Liam will do everything in his power to protect both his brother and Alec from the wolves, even if it means calling in favors and killing those with whom he once ran.

Because Alec, like it or not, is Liam's chosen mate.

Warning, this title contains the following: explicit male/male sex.

Available now in ebook and print from Samhain Publishing.

GREAT
CHEAP
FUN

Discover eBooks!

THE FASTEST WAY TO GET THE HOTTEST NAMES

Get your favorite authors on your favorite reader, long before they're out in print! Ebooks from Samhain go wherever you go, and work with whatever you carry—Palm, PDF, Mobi, and more.

WWW.SAMHAINPUBLISHING.COM

Lightning Source UK Ltd.
Milton Keynes UK
18 August 2009

142808UK00001B/166/P